The Sea Rose

LORDS AND LADIES OF THE SEA
BOOK ONE

MARIELLA HUNT

WWW.MARIELLAHUNT.COM

Cover design by Mariella Hunt

Interior Design by M. H. Woodscourt

www.mariellahunt.com

ISBN (Paperback): 9798362105778

To Mom, Dad, and my brother—
This book is for you.

And to my readers in the Vella community—
My heartfelt thanks.

One

When a song was beautiful, the notes on its sheet of music hummed with life. Lord Peter West sat at the piano, seeking refuge in his late father's favorite sonata. He played a chord, allowing its hum to fill the music room. The sound soaked through to his strangled soul.

Peter heard the buzz of servants at work. He noticed changes—a dusted shelf, rearranged pottery, signs of rooms well-tended. The servants, though meant to be silent, contributed to the orchestra of the Everly estate. He could not tune them out.

Peter wished his father's spirit would make a sound, instead—wished he could ask if he had made the correct decision and hear a whispered *yes* or *no*. However, David West, Earl of Everly, was dead—had died, leaving Peter alone to face a daunting future.

Though Peter never entertained thoughts of marrying for love, he didn't imagine that an impending engagement would bring such dread.

Gazing at the piano, he searched the reflection for a

message. He sought reassurance that, one day, life would be more than a matter of duty.

Everly was large. If he never found love for Lady Meredith, they could have their own rooms. He needn't see her every day. Life could continue as it had always been; only his bachelor status would have changed.

"Peter!" His sister, Sybil, pulled him from his reverie, her voice ringing down the corridor.

She stepped into the music room, more grace and cheer in her step than he could muster. "We're about to leave. The carriage is ready."

Peter reached for the piano lid, lowering it to cover the keys. He let out a breath and said, "Very well. I will meet you shortly."

Sybil stood at the arched doorway. Rarely did she leave the mansion without dressing well, but for this ball, she had outdone herself. Her auburn hair was braided and adorned with silver combs; she wore a gown of soft peach, as welcoming as her personality.

"I wish you would smile," Sybil told him, stepping nearer. "Surely you are experiencing nerves."

Peter stood, sliding the piano bench into place.

Sybil must be right. He would survive the evening and sleep into the afternoon. A few weeks later, he would be married. Then, he could retreat to his library and pore over Father's books.

Or he could sit in the shadows of bookshelves and allow himself to finish grieving.

Again, Sybil read his thoughts.

"Father's here," she said, placing a hand on his arm, "I am certain of it! I would have liked to have him at my wedding, too, one day." She shrugged her shoulders. "I do not allow myself to believe his love has vanished."

Peter smiled. It was difficult to ignore his sister's optimism.

"No," he said, taking her hand and giving it a squeeze. "His love will not have vanished. I believe that all will be well, Sybil. I might need time to adjust to the world as it is. There is an emptiness where he ought to be."

Sybil nodded. "Such is grief," she said.

Hoping to end the conversation on that note, Peter forced spring into his step.

As the heir, he could not afford to be choosy. This wedding would unite two strong families, which would benefit the estate.

Sybil's marriage would be an occasion for joy. He would make sure that, when she married, it was to a man who made her happy. If the glow ever faded from her expression, he would know it was the wrong person.

His little sister would never feel trapped as he did now.

They stepped into the warm June afternoon. He glanced over his shoulder at the impressive height of Everly Mansion, carved of white stone and punctuated with Greek columns. It was his father's pride and joy. Peter would make this sacrifice to maintain the legacy Lord David West so carefully cultivated.

Mother waited in the carriage, having shed her black mourning clothes for the lavender of half-mourning. With tense gloved hands, she clutched a jeweled reticule.

She appraised Peter as he took the seat next to Sybil. "At last," she said. "You can't afford to be the only person late to the ball."

"The guests have been waiting three months," Peter said, unapologetic. "They can wait another hour."

Sybil giggled, stifling the sound with the back of her hand. Peter smirked and turned to the window as the carriage began to move.

The grassy fields rolled on, the pond in front of their home sparkled blue in the sunlight. These things would not change, even with a loveless marriage. If he could only get through the social events and ceremony, he would return to the peace of his yard.

The thought consoled him during the ride. He hoped he could keep such poise when faced with guests and dancing.

THOUGH THEY WERE NOT late by much, Mother wore a scowl when they arrived at Lord Bannister's country home.

Guests stood in the colorful garden, escaping the stifling warmth indoors. Lady Meredith Bannister, to whom he would be wed, stood entertaining a handful of friends. They had all chosen bold colors in an attempt to outdo one another. The guests shifted and flailed in their efforts to catch attention.

For all of his misgivings, Peter could not deny that Lady Meredith needed no theatrics to catch attention. With her poise and striking features, he imagined she would be stunning in sackcloth.

Peter would be a fool to deny her beauty, but he must have been damaged by grief. Though he recognized that many gentlemen would have been glad to take his place, Lady Meredith did not cause his heart to race.

She wore a blue-and-white day dress. She held a white

lace fan to protect her face from the sun, her skin already free of blemish. Her hair, blonde-almost-silver, was worn in a knot at the nape of her neck. She smiled at something her friend said, a twitch of lips that did not say whether she found the *something* to be funny.

As the West carriage came into view, Meredith lowered the fan and glanced in their direction. Her steely eyes broke the initial enchantment her loveliness set on him.

You are late, said those eyes.

How similar she was to Mother. Perhaps that was why he could not fall for her.

Conversation hushed as footmen helped Peter, Sybil, and Mother out of the carriage. Every person in the crowd stared at him. He knew that they suspected an announcement would take place. They anticipated it like wolves awaiting their next meal.

Fresh gossip for them, fresh meat! So-and-so's fashion disaster would fade from public memory; yesterday's scandal would evaporate in the shadow of this, the wedding of the year…

Lady Meredith and her gaggle of companions came near to greet the Wests. Gone was the steel he had seen in her eyes; for Sybil and Mother, she became the face of charisma.

"How splendid that you've come," she said, curtsying. The ladies behind her did the same, a rustle of skirts, a flash of hair combs. "We began to worry of an accident. The path can be treacherous if you are unfamiliar with the roads."

Mother remained silent. Peter understood: Being the reason for their lateness, he was to make conversation.

"Enjoying them, more like," he said with a bow. "The scenery is splendid."

"Yes," agreed Meredith. "Father chose this place because

5

it is peaceful and out of the way. He is glad to open it for guests today, though."

"Where is Lord Bannister?" Sybil asked, offering Peter time to gather his wits for the next exchange. "Shall we greet him?"

"He is in the gallery," said Meredith. "Follow me."

Leaving her colorful crowd in the garden, she led the guests to the poignant place that was Bannister House.

Peter fell into step with her, but could not find words to say. Perhaps it was best not to fill his mouth with empty talk. He would say enough when giving the speech, and preferred to save his breath.

"You look striking," he did say. It was true, and polite enough.

Meredith did not spare him a glance. "Thank you," she said with a wave of her fan. "I have been told that four times today."

Peter winced, and did not try again to make conversation.

LORD LIONEL WHITBY, Earl Bannister, had invited everybody who was anybody to witness this speech. All of the guests were eager for the dancing to commence.

Music began as the evening set in.

Peter and Meredith stepped out for the first set; other couples fell into place behind them. Song floated over the guests in the ballroom, making colors brighter, adding sparkle to a smile.

Peter watched Sybil throughout the night, paying attention to the gentlemen who asked her for a dance. He discerned those who basked in her glow, discarding any who appeared more interested in flashing their own qualities. One of these men might one day ask for his sister's hand. He intended to make an educated choice.

"You are distracted," said Meredith, when an hour passed in this manner. Though she spoke quietly, he managed to hear her voice over the violin.

Peter smiled an apology at her. "I'm keeping an eye on my sister."

Meredith's smile did not reach her eyes; indeed, there was something odd, uncharacteristic anxiety in the way she watched him.

"I would not understand," she said. "I have no siblings."

"Sybil will be your sister," he pointed out.

"Yes." Again, distracted. "You should make the speech after the next dance."

Peter could not help but frown. "Are you well?"

He could not remember seeing Lady Meredith nervous. Gone was her poise. She stared at him, he suspected, to avoid looking somewhere else.

"Impatient to have it done with," she said, clearing her throat. "Make the speech before everyone is drunk. Let there be no place for questioning."

The manner in which she spoke caused his spirits to sour. He had rehearsed every word, but disliked being commanded as though he were a servant.

"I will make the speech when the moment is right," he said.

She responded in a rush: "We spoke of this. The purpose of the ball is to confirm..."

"Lady Meredith, hours remain in which I can say those words. Allow me to choose."

She inhaled, glanced over her shoulder. "It seems like a waste of time to me." There was a quiver in her words.

Her sudden panic caused him sympathy. Of course, she was a lady. A fitting engagement might be the most important thing to happen to her. He understood why she did not want to wait.

"After the next dance," he said, and her relief was visible.

"Yes?" she prompted, a loaded question. He sensed more behind the word than a wish for confirmation. Something, indeed, had put her on edge.

"Yes," he said. *They are only words, I can speak as if on a stage.* "But your father must begin the speech."

It would be awkward to address the people; he would prefer it if Lord Bannister arranged things beforehand.

"Very well." Words spilled from her mouth. "I shall tell him and return."

Peter said nothing as she slipped into the crowd. He wondered about her anxiety, but bristled at being told what to do.

Reminding himself that the night was nearly finished, he went in search of water.

LADY MEREDITH WAS KNOWN to be a graceful dancer. He had never seen her stumble through a set, even when tired, even in a crowded room. That night, her sudden fear did not change this. However, her demeanor remained tense as they made their way through a set.

Peter listened to the music, trying to wring confidence from its melody. It would have be easier to make the announcement if Meredith hadn't changed so drastically.

He had an unpleasant suspicion that the speech was no longer about a union between two families. What it actually was, he could not say.

Meredith gripped his shoulder tightly enough that he knew she would leave a bruise.

"If you would tell me what is wrong," he whispered, cringing, "then perhaps—"

She cut him off. "Nothing is wrong."

"I don't believe you."

Meredith looked up and snapped, "Nothing is wrong! It's been a long night and I want that speech to be made *now*."

Peter pulled away. He did not consider himself a proud man, but would like to be treated with kindness, especially since Lady Meredith was begging for him to make an announcement in front of influential people.

Did he not deserve a smile? Gentle words, at least? If she could not manage to say *please* on this pivotal night, he did not know if he could bear a life with her.

The music stopped shortly after he backed away. Meredith stared at him with alarm, surely knowing that her words had gone too far.

"I will have a moment, then," he said, hearing ice in his words, "to make myself *want* to speak."

Meredith opened her mouth, but no words came.

Peter stormed to a nearby balcony. He stepped out, inhaling the mild air. Red velvet curtains shielded him from view.

He lifted his face to the skies, seeking the stars that made up Orion's Belt. His father had taught him about constellations; Peter had many fond memories of stretching out on the grass with Father, talking about philosophy and astronomy.

His hands trembled, so he clasped them behind his back.

If Peter could consult with his father, what would Lord David West tell him to do? Would he be like Mother, insisting that Peter make a pleasing match—even if the woman cut him with her words?

Peter remembered the last time he went walking with her. Meredith had repeated like a general how this ball was expected to end. She reminded him what a failure he would be if his speech did not portray her as the love of his life.

"Your mother told me you have expressed doubts," Meredith said that day, her voice devoid of emotion. "I know you feel sad about the death of your father, but you cannot let grief paralyze your life. The mourning period is over."

Peter had been floored by the mention of his father. He ought to have said that David West's death was not related to his hesitance, but Meredith continued before he had time.

"Everything will play out according to plan," said Meredith that day, her words a threat rather than reassurance. "Imagine the pride your father would feel when you made a match to honor his legacy!"

Peter pulled his arm from hers, angered that she should use Father in this affair. "Lady Meredith—"

"*Lady* Meredith? Dear, you must practice dropping formalities."

The poisoned honey dripping from her mouth as she called him *dear* would kill a man; Peter marveled that he had not died. Perhaps he had no life left in him to lose.

"Me—Meredith," Peter had said, uncomfortable with the thought of treating her by her Christian name. "My father—"

"Imagine how disappointed he would be if things did *not* work out," said Lady Meredith. If she heard his anger, she chose to ignore it. "I imagine he would be rolling in his grave."

Peter had been so enraged that he could think of no response.

Days later, alone on the balcony and moments from the announcement, peace washed over him as the answer became clear.

He might not have forgotten the speech he composed; it did not matter. He wouldn't have been able to say the words.

It was not the right match. Peter would not make the speech.

He slipped inside, concealing himself behind the curtain. Lord Bannister had gathered his guests in conversation, fueling excitement for the moment he expected to take place. Mother stood by his side with Sybil, while Lady Meredith exchanged pleasantries with an acquaintance.

He wiped his sweaty palms together, wondering if he would regret taking the coward's way out. Was it the coward's way out, though, if his fear was true? He could not agree to a marriage when it was difficult for him to breathe.

The heat of the stuffy ballroom increased his desperation.

Peter spotted an exit across from him and made a quick choice.

Lord Bannister had begun an anecdote about a Half-Mer woman he crossed paths with during a trip to London.

"She was told politely that London isn't a place for people like her to shop," he said with indignation. "To which she replied that she was aware, but did not care."

"I thought that they had shops," said a woman behind him.

"They do, but that is not enough. They clamor for a day when their children and ours can mingle." Bannister shook his head. "A sad day that would be, exposing our sons and daughters to people with little regard for morality…"

The crowd listened, rapt, to Bannister's speech. They did not notice Peter slipping away from the balcony, darting into the corridor.

Relief washed over him as he spotted the stairs, and the front door beyond them.

Peter hesitated, wondering if he ought to tell Sybil why there would be no speech. Sybil talked too much, though, at social events; he did not trust her to remain quiet for long enough for him to get home. It was his mistake for having taken so long to come to a solution, and he would settle matters later about his timing.

He did not understand Meredith's behavior, but knew that she was not going to be reasonable. He would face her later, as well—explain his disappearance someplace private, where he was not forced to make a performance in front of guests.

"Now," said Lord Bannister, his tone becoming one of cheer, "it is a delight for me to share news regarding my daughter and the esteemed Lord Everly. Where is he, darling?"

Peter hurried down the stairs, taking care not to make noise. He had reached the first landing when he heard Meredith's voice.

"Peter?"

He stiffened and turned. Given no other choice, he would have to face her now.

Meredith descended with poise. He stepped back; the blades in her eyes pierced him. He could not remember how to move but longed for the strength to descend the final set of stairs.

"I hope you are here to finish composing yourself," Meredith said, moving so close that a misstep would cause him to tumble. "Should I find smelling salts?"

Peter's voice trembled as he formed one word: "No."

"No?" Meredith attempted to wear her aloof mask—he knew she was trying to distance herself enough to sound annoyed.

If not for the panic stiffening her shoulders, he might have believed she was angry. If not for the madness he saw behind her eyes.

"Are you a *child?*" she demanded.

"No," he said. Then, finding courage, "I am not going to marry you."

The daggers in her eyes vanished. "Perhaps you need fifteen more minutes," she said, a quiver in her voice. "Or a glass of whisky."

"No," he repeated. "I'm young and I have time to choose. I intend to grow old with someone who cares for more than her own self-importance."

Meredith took a step back.

They stared at one another, Peter shocked that he'd dared to voice how he felt. In the ballroom, a confused hum rose from the guests.

"You can't change your mind now," Meredith whispered. "I know you are confused, perhaps unwell. We can make the announcement another day, if you like—"

"I am not a child," Peter said, pronouncing each word as if she were the child. "There will be no wedding. No one will make this choice for me. I wish you the best of luck, Meredith."

Her breath came in unsteady gasps. He felt a prickling on the back of his neck, a warning, a whisper of fear.

"I will ask you now to step aside," he said. "I want to get home and write—"

"You are a fool," she hissed, madness darkening her beautiful features—madness and something else.

Meredith lunged forward. Peter did not move fast enough to dodge the shove.

He felt the battering on his body as he tumbled down the stairs. Acting on impulse, he reached in every direction until he managed to grasp one of the railings, ears ringing.

He forced himself off of the ground, breaking into a run. He did not have the clarity of mind to hear what Meredith shouted as he stumbled out of the door.

There was something hot and sticky on his sleeve; was he injured? No matter. That could be tended to when he was someplace else—anywhere else—

He limped into the stable and found the horses that brought his family's carriage. Reaching for the one nearest, he tried but failed to remember what she was called.

Ignoring the questions of the stableboy, Peter mounted the horse and kicked her into a gallop. He rode into the darkness, his mind a haze of pain and confusion.

As the night swallowed him in his escape, he hoped that, somewhere, Father might be proud of him.

Peter knew his mother would be furious. Even Sybil would ask why he did not reclaim his freedom in a dignified manner.

What story would Meredith tell regarding his disappearance? She would not allow herself to be painted as a fool.

Before he could tell his truth, she would spread word of how badly he insulted her.

Peter could not go home. However, he hadn't the slightest idea of where he was to stop for the night.

If he could only stay awake…if he could get his thoughts straight…

Two

Rose Finch choked on a bitter tang of smoke as she navigated familiar passages, taking quick strides, hugging a bag to her chest. People ignored her as she passed, mumbling to one another.

Dalton, chided a familiar voice in her head. Your surname is Dalton. Rose ignored it; when Father died, she and her mother shed his family name. For years, Rose used her father's title of Finch as a surname instead, attempting to separate herself from the past. Now everybody called her Miss Rose Finch.

Lady Rose Dalton, daughter of the late Earl Finch, remained dormant in her memory. His surname, Dalton, was an echo shoved away with the rest of her past.

The marketplace teemed with nervous energy. It did not matter how many local homes went up in flames: Each attack brought fresh panic. Rose was glad for it, in a way; the people of Blue Cora district never ceased to care for one another. They stood together against the *polite society*.

People of the upper crust considered Merpeople and

their descendants immoral, like sirens of myth. They judged without knowing the integrity of the ocean-blooded. Until one of the nobility deigned to converse with one of them, the Merpeople would forever be made out as monsters.

Rose could not remember having met a Merman or Mermaid who wished they didn't have ocean-blood. Sometimes the Mer-scales ~~were~~ caused frustration when they grew on obvious places, such as a person's face. Even folk with that luck did not curse their heritage.

Rose stumbled into the bakery, taking a deep breath of fresh air. The scent of fresh loaves reminded her that she hadn't eaten a bite since her meager breakfast of porridge that morning. She was always able to get through the day without noticing hunger; it was not until nighttime that the sensation set in.

Shaking her head, she pressed on with the chore, hurrying to the counter. She was relieved to find Natasha tending to customers. As a former resident of Mrs. Whittle's orphanage, Natasha was one of few people Rose considered to be a friend.

Rose had not been born in this district and struggled to make friends. She found it easier to interact with ladies who had grown up in Mrs. Whittle's care. They treated her like family, because they shared a childhood.

Mrs. Whittle's ladies remained loyal to their mistress long after they moved on in life.

Natasha beamed as Rose neared the counter. "The usual?"

"Yes, please," Rose said. "We're out again."

"Oh," Natasha said, sadness in her tone. "I was hoping our last donation would be more helpful."

"It lasted for as long as it could have," Rose assured her, smiling. "But growing girls do eat."

Rose did not admit to having given her rations to Anne, the youngest. An unspoken rule among Mrs. Whittle's charges was that the young held priority.

"Do you know whose house it is this time?" Rose inquired, looking at the window. Only a thin pane of glass separated them from the smoke.

"It's Tim Hardy's house," Natasha said unhappily, selecting eight rolls and placing them in Rose's bag. "So grim. I heard whispers that the baby didn't survive. Of course, they could be words of panic circulating, but…" She shrugged. "Such rumors do not spring without fodder. I suppose we'll learn in the morning."

Rose was prepared to believe it; the innocent did not survive the smoke of hatred and fear. Mrs. Hardy had been so proud of her baby boy, bringing him to the church service and introducing him to friends.

She dug coins out of a small, battered purse, trying not to think of where they would acquire money the next day.

In seasons such as these, desperate measures were taken. Cook had been dismissed, her cot in the basement empty as she had returned to live with her aunt. She would be sent for when there were groceries for a full meal. Meanwhile, Rose and Marie made do with what they had, creating soups that gave the illusion of being full.

Handing the coins to Natasha, Rose said, "Stay safe—and please visit. We would love company, even if we can't offer refreshments."

Natasha accepted the coins, beaming. "I'll bring refreshments. Tell Mrs. Whittle I say hello."

Rose nodded.

With reluctance, she stepped back into the smoky night. She spoke to no one as she navigated the passages to the orphanage.

Hiding from view was not difficult, since no one paid her any heed. The few remaining pedestrians gathered in tight circles. She sensed they were sharing the same dark whisper, bemoaning that an innocent should have died in a fire.

~

THE ORPHANAGE WAS SITUATED at the edge of the district. Rose suspected that this nearness to 'proper' society was the only thing saving it from being torched. It was in a spot prominent to *fully human* neighbors, which meant an act of arson would be seen.

Fires could only remain ignored by the government if kept out of sight.

Familiar men kept watch on street corners, some holding knives. They called themselves the night watch, and took their positions religiously at sunset. Each man hoped to capture the people responsible for the fires, convinced that they could not slip away unnoticed forever.

When the culprit was caught, Rose predicted a fearsome act of local justice. The night watch would ensure that the culprits suffered, much like the people they had killed or made homeless.

Old Jimmy was stationed by the orphanage that night. His gray hair suggested advanced age, but appearances were misleading. The passing years hadn't weakened him; he defended his people with a passion that Rose found inspiring.

"That was quick," he said, spotting Rose. "When Meril goes shopping, I always expect her to get caught in a chat with somebody."

"It isn't a day to chat," Rose said. "There's another fire. It's the Hardy home this time, and it appears that the baby did not survive."

Jimmy cursed under his breath. "There'll be a funeral tomorrow," he said, "and I wager everyone will attend."

"I'll be there, and so will the girls. Please be careful—the arsonists might not be gone. I need to get this bread to the girls."

Jimmy nodded, in his rage unable to form another word. Rose left him to his anger, anxious to complete her task.

Mrs. Whittle's Orphanage was a handsome home with character in every beam of wood. It was not dank as one might expect when hearing the word *orphan;* the ladies residing there never felt unloved.

The orphanage had been a place of refuge for Rose and her mother. After Father's murder, there was no question of their staying in the great country house. Mrs. Whittle, an old friend of Mother's, was happy to offer them shelter and work. After Mother fell ill and died, Rose had already learned to call the place home.

Rose slowed her pace, waiting for her heart to settle. She did not want to be hysterical when presenting the bread, nor did she want to alarm the girls overmuch. If there was a funeral in the morning, Mrs. Whittle would have them up early, and they needed to get their sleep.

Smoke invaded her breath. It served as a reminder that, as she stood safely at the door to the orphanage, another family watched their life become ash.

Rose paused at the door, sobered by the thought. She

could allow herself a moment of grief before going inside. If she felt it before entering, it would be spent, and she could speak to the girls with a steady tone.

From the corner of her eye she caught a glimpse of movement. Turning, she heard herself cry in surprise, *"Oh!"*

A shadow ambled from behind the house. Rose waited until her eyes adjusted to make out the shape—it was a horse.

The black steed wandered with great fear. Spotting her, it trotted in her direction.

There was dark poetry in having a black horse step from the shadows on such an unfortunate day. Rose felt superstition became stronger than the logic she taught the orphans.

"Jimmy!" she called. "There's a horse here!"

The horse whinnied. Struck by its urgency, her eyes followed its path. It trotted in three circles and dipped its head to nudge something on the ground. Light spilled from a nearby window, allowing her to spot a person unconscious on the grass, concealed by shadow.

Rose heard Jimmy approach and allowed her shoulders to relax. She placed her parcel of bread on the grass and crept towards the figure. He wore a fine suit, the mark of someone with money. His face was turned down, making it difficult to gauge an age.

Placing a hand on his neck, she was relieved to find a pulse. She would not have been able to stomach another death.

Jimmy shone a lantern over the man, revealing an angry wound on the stranger's head. He must have fallen off of the horse in a moment of exhaustion.

Uneasy questions settled in her mind.

Why would a moneyed gentleman be riding through

Cora, tonight of all nights? Those of his class pretended that the Mer did not exist, acknowledging them only when making plans to keep them out of sight.

"Curious, this," Jimmy said, kneeling beside her. "What's one of the gentry doing here? On the night of a fire, no doubt."

His words gave her a chill. "Surely you don't think him responsible for it," she said, not willing to believe that the stranger could set fire to a home.

"Don't you think it odd?" Jimmy's voice had no compassion. "'Course, I never thought it might be a rich person doing it. They wouldn't spare us the time to strike a match on our homes. But we can't be too careful in keeping our own safe, don't you think?"

Rose shook her head. "Let him wake up first," she said. "Don't make him a suspect when he is out cold."

The man's fine clothing had been tailored to his figure, though his jacket and trousers were dirty and torn. His blond hair bore evidence of having been greased and styled before the fall. Checking the cufflinks on his coat, her eyes widened at a glint of gold.

"We need to get him inside," she said. "Otherwise, he'll wind up dead or robbed."

Jimmy had been eyeing the cufflinks with poorly veiled greed. Those bits of gold could have keep him and his wife fed for months. "What of the horse?"

"Ask the Moores if they can keep it in their stable. I'm going to tell Mrs. Whittle about this gentleman—please try to wake him."

MRS. WHITTLE WAS in the sitting room, reading by the fireplace. She looked up at Rose's sudden entrance. "Why, girl, you're pale as a sheet! What ever has happened?"

"There's been an accident outside of the orphanage, ma'am," said Rose. "A gentleman must have gotten lost and fallen off of his horse. He's unconscious with a wound on his head. Can we bring him inside until he wakes?"

She was silent, for the moment, about Jimmy's suspicion. If sense was not talked into him, a deadly rumor would reach the locals by morning. Mobs intent on vengeance would waste no time tearing the stranger to bits.

She would not think about it yet; first, he needed to come inside.

Mrs. Whittle stood. "This is an orphanage for young ladies—it wouldn't be proper."

Rose heard the hesitance in her words. Mrs. Whittle had a protective shell, but inside of that shell, her heart was generous. The matron of this orphanage would never let anyone bleed to death outside of her door, propriety be damned.

"We must allow him to sleep somewhere, at least for one night," Rose insisted, placing the bag of bread on a chair. "He might be well enough to leave by sunrise. You know the people here would steal from him."

Or they might blame him for something awful and kill him. This Rose did not say out loud, but she knew Mrs. Whittle was thinking the same thing. The woman was sensible; surely she would not be like Jimmy, condemning a man before he stopped bleeding.

"Or worse," agreed Mrs. Whittle. "The gentleman may rest in the cellar until he's stable. He can borrow Cook's cot. Let me find some blankets." She paused. "Be careful that the girls do not learn of his presence. Dress his wounds quietly."

"Yes, ma'am." Rose wondered if the gentleman would take offense at being cured by one of the Mer. "Jimmy can help me get him downstairs."

And I will remind him to be silent—at least until we know who the man is.

"I'll be upstairs while the girls take tea," Mrs. Whittle said. "Tonight, I shall make them say all of their prayers; that ought to keep them in place."

ROSE STEPPED ONCE MORE into the mild air. Jimmy had helped the gentleman up to a sitting position. In the light of the lantern she saw he was not much older than herself.

His eyes darted towards Rose as she approached; dazed, he shut them quickly. He might have been moving, but they were the movements of a man trapped in a dream.

"Mrs. Whittle says he can stay in the cellar," said Rose. "Please help me bring him in."

Despite his hunched shoulders, Jimmy demonstrated impressive strength during manual work. He helped the young man to his feet while Rose took the gentleman's arm.

In the most soothing voice she could muster, she told him, "We'll get you someplace to rest, sir. Can you understand me?"

He turned, staring with enough depth that she knew he was seeing her. Light from Jimmy's lantern shone on his face, revealing it in detail.

A memory stirred at the sight of his countenance—the sky-blue eyes with tired dark circles, the pointed shape of his nose. Could it be that she had known this man in her former life? She had played with a great many upper-class children before Father's death.

"Yes," he croaked, "I understand." He did not appear to recognize her.

Rose continued to stare until Jimmy cleared his throat, forcing her to concentrate. They guided the man into the orphanage, steering him into the cellar, where Jimmy eased him into the cot. The man groaned with discomfort when resting his head, causing her heart to sink with sympathy.

Rose placed the lamp on a nearby crate and hurried upstairs, where Mrs. Whittle handed her a pile of folded blankets. The woman pursed her lips, reminding Rose with her eyes: *Be quiet about this.*

Hugging the blankets, Rose nodded. "Good night."

"Good night, Rose," said Mrs. Whittle, and she made her way up the stairs, her steps remarkably steady.

Once alone, Rose pondered the situation. It had been years since she reflected on how life had been before Father's murder. The effort of adjusting to new surroundings did not push memories of a comfortable life from her mind. Instead, they lurked in the shadows of her grief, emerging when she could not sleep.

At the sight of the wounded man, these memories struggled from their dormancy. She did not know how to usher them away; they clouded her thoughts, imparing her judgment.

Rose returned to the cellar slowly. It was cooler than the rest of the house; she hoped this would make the man comfortable as he recovered.

Jimmy had helped him out of his coat; a quick look reassured Rose that the cufflinks remained in place. She trusted

Jimmy to protect the lives of her pupils, but a person in desperation did not often resist easy plunder.

"Thank you, Jimmy," said Rose, placing the pillow under her patient's head. He did not protest, appearing to have passed out. "I'll take it from here."

"He didn't say anything while you were gone," said Jimmy. "That blow to his head was a nasty one. I wouldn't be surprised if it wiped his memory."

Rose bit her lip; she had nursed people to health before, but never thought she'd find herself tending to someone with amnesia.

"Will you return tomorrow?" she asked. "In case we need help. He might be more comfortable talking to a man."

Jimmy smiled ironically. "Sure, but don't tell him what I am. 'Fact, I wouldn't tell him where he is at all. One of his lot would rather die than be found among us."

Rose cringed at the thought of deception, but knew it to be true. No one wanted to be near the Mer—not the gentry, not the middle-class, not even the 'pure-blooded poor'.

"I'll give it thought," she promised. "Have a good night. And please, don't tell anyone about him. We need to learn who he is before we blame him for a crime—don't you agree?"

"I'll hold back on a verdict until I can speak to him. When we brought him downstairs, I noticed no scent of smoke on his clothing. It gave me cause to doubt his involvement." Jimmy crossed his arms, appraising the man. "But it does not explain his presence, and we cannot assume him to be a friend. You're young, Miss Rose, and have a good heart, but those of us with ocean-blood cannot trust an outsider."

Rose accepted his words to be true: Merpeople could

trust no person that did not share their heritage. She was thankful for Jimmy's prudence and hoped that suitable reasons would be offered for this man's presence.

"Until tomorrow, then," she said with a smile.

"Until tomorrow. Be careful, Miss—he might be unconscious, but that doesn't mean he would not attack if startled."

With a quick bow, Jimmy turned and hurried up the stairs.

Rose returned her attention to her patient. Deep in unconsciousness, he did not move. Moving to an empty crate, she allowed herself a moment to sit and gather her wits.

Between the burning of the Hardy home and this mysterious man, the exhaustion was overwhelming. Tears threatened to emerge, but she held them back.

Rose stared at his beaten face, eyes narrowing in thought. *Where have I seen him before?*

An idea struck her. Sliding off the crate and onto her knees, she reached for his hand and was relieved to find that he wore a signet ring.

Bringing the lantern closer, she made out the image: It was the initial *W* rising from a wave, as if itself part of the water.

Rose heard herself gasp as she dropped his hand. He stirred without waking.

There was no need to disturb him, for she knew what his name was. The battered young man on the cot was Peter West, son of her late father's business partner, Lord David, Earl of Everly.

Peter's ring answered most of her questions. The letter *W* was for their surname; the waves represented their family legacy of great ships. All that remained to be asked was *why* Lord Everly's son was unconscious on their lawn.

Then came his voice, muffled and unclear as he emerged from a stupor: "Wh—where am I?"

Rose forced herself to look at Peter West. He stared back, showing no signs of recognition.

What would she tell him? Did she have the strength to lie to him about his whereabouts? She could not justify keeping the truth from him.

"Hello," was all that she managed. "I'm going to wash your wound."

Three

"MY WOUND?" PETER REPEATED, PUZZLED.

"Yes," replied the young woman. "You fell from the horse and took a blow to your head."

As if to confirm her claim, a sharp pain flared on the side of his head. On impulse, he reached up to touch it—only for her to grasp his wrist, stopping him.

"Leave it," she said. "It needs washing and time to heal."

He stared at the small, calloused hand. It was the hand of a working woman, unlike the manicured ladies he was acquainted with.

Abruptly, she released him, as though she had been holding something hot and noticed too late. Peter could still feel her touch after she moved away.

The manner in which she'd grabbed him stirred a deep emotion in him. She stopped him from touching the wound to prevent his making it worse, to protect him. The last person to place a hand on him had shoved him down a flight of stairs.

Peter chanced a look at his surroundings. He was in a

dark but not uncomfortable room, lying on a cot. It was not his feather bed, yet he relished the comfort, bone-weary. A lantern flickered, threatening to make him nod off again.

Peter wondered how much time had passed since his escape from the Bannister home. How long had he been unconscious on the grass?

Now, a strange woman watched him with concern. Meredith hadn't cared for him, before or after the fall; this stranger promised to heal him.

Meredith grasped his arm to bruise him; this person did so to protect him.

"The injury needs cleaning before it becomes infected," she explained. "Wait here while I fetch water and towels. Brace yourself, sir. It will sting."

He nodded but said nothing. Physical pain did not compare to what he'd endured in a year of loveless courtship.

Falling from a horse might make him sore for a while; the wounds Meredith inflicted were different. He could think of no remedy for her jabs about his father, her insults at his timidity, or the way she told him what to do while never approving in the end. His own mother was no better. She had taken to commanding him as if he were the family dog.

As the woman got to her feet, fatigue crept over him. He closed his eyes and listened to her ascend the stairs. Despite the throbbing in his temples, it was pleasant in this cellar.

He preferred the silence to a string quartet. He preferred being injured on a cot to dancing for others' approval.

He preferred not knowing where he was—because no one here knew who he was.

"Sir?" Her voice pulled him back to the waking world.

Peter opened his eyes, determined to be friendlier than he had been at the start.

He hadn't noted the woman's looks before. Now he took in the details of her appearance, a difficult task in the muted lamplight. Her brown hair was pulled into a knot from which had escaped an unruly lock. Peter watched her bat it out of her vision as she settled onto the ground, holding a basin of water and towels.

"I'm sorry to wake you," she told him, "but it's best to clean the wound before you sleep. I spoke to the home-owner, Mrs. Whittle. You're welcome to stay until you recover."

"I won't recover," he heard himself say, words slipping before he could halt them.

Blast, he thought, attempting to regain control. *It's not her concern.*

"Why?" she asked. "Do you think you've broken a rib?"

"No," he slurred. "No broken ribs."

The woman tilted her head with curiosity. "Can you tell me your name, sir?"

There was something odd in her voice. She demonstrated undisguised interest in hearing him speak his name.

Before he could inquire about it, she added, "I ask to discard the possibility of memory loss. With a head injury, there's that danger."

Peter shook his head, ignoring the pain it caused him. He did not want to say his name in this cool, safe room. He wanted to be a stranger. He wanted to vanish into the shadows.

He suffered from no memory loss; the events of the Bannister ball remained crystal-clear in his mind. Meredith's strange behavior, how she begged for him to make the speech early. The row, the remark she made that caused him to lose patience.

Peter remembered standing behind the curtain, struggling to understand what *he* wanted from life. Could he marry that woman? The answer had been no. It was an epiphany which might have come late, but it brought him peace.

After that, Peter felt confident in his decision for one entire minute. He should have hurried out without delay. He should not have stopped to ponder explaining his choice to Sybil.

Had he been gone seconds earlier, Meredith would not have found him at the stairs. He would not have encountered a woman with wild eyes who would not listen to reason.

He would not have seen her fear and anger before she shoved him.

He would not be lost.

"Sir?" the woman asked. "Your name."

"Blast my name," he said, to which she frowned.

"If you have lost your memory, I need to know. I cannot treat a patient without knowing the symptoms."

"Tell me yours first."

He regretted his words when her face fell. All she'd asked for was a name, and he responded with a command, as if she were a maid working in his house. It made him sound too much like his mother, unfeeling, condescending.

"Sorry," Peter said. "I don't know—how to form a coherent sentence."

"*Your name,*" she said, this time not a question but a demand.

Using a tone that he hoped conveyed remorse, he said, "My name is Peter West."

He omitted his title, not wanting to be *Lord Peter West* anymore. *Lord Peter West* was a rich girl's plaything. No one respected *Lord Peter West* before he ran off; they certainly wouldn't now. Let it be said that the young Earl of Everly died after a fall down the stairs.

Lord Peter West was never destined for happiness. Perhaps *just Peter* could build a new life and find a semblance of peace.

The woman closed her eyes upon hearing his name, something like anguish in her expression. She did not give him time to understand her reaction. "Do you remember the moment you fell off of the horse?"

"Vaguely." Peter tried propping himself up on his elbows, but the room began to spin. Accepting that he was too injured to sit, he rested his head on the pillow. "I remember clinging to her as I slipped."

"A neighbor is caring for your horse while you stay." The young lady did not meet his gaze, focused on dipping a towel in the basin of water.

Was Peter imagining the manner in which she leaned away from him? Had he angered her with his reluctance to reveal his name?

She flung another question at him. "Do you remember anything that happened before the injury?"

"I remember—"

Peter's voice cracked. He recalled the sensation of falling, that helpless fraction of a second after Meredith's shove. He remembered terror as he flew in midair with nothing to grab. Then came pain when he hit the stairs and began to slide, *bang bang bang* step after step, until he managed to clutch a railing and break the momentum.

Memories returned with such force that the event could have been repeating itself.

Tears prickled at his eyes. All he managed was a whisper: "I remember."

Peter wiped at the tears, angry with himself, and waited for more questions. Instead there was silence; he heard no sound except for the woman's breathing and his racing heart.

He was caught in midair, helpless.

He longed to be alone so he could bat those memories off, the way this woman kept batting at her lock of hair.

She said, "I'm going to begin washing. Are you ready?"

"Yes," he choked, grateful for a reason to stop talking.

This was no longer a safe room; his recollections left a trail by which his fears had traced him. He did not know how to stop crying in front of this stranger.

What would Father think?

The young lady spoke in a soothing tone as she wiped his wound with a towel (he winced, but his inner turmoil was greater).

"I was told to hide this," she said, "but you have a right to know your whereabouts. Sir, you are in one of the Mer districts. You fell on the lawn of a young ladies' orphanage. Now you are in the orphanage's cellar."

She stopped dabbing at the wound, waiting for a reaction.

A pause ensued as her words sank in. Peter had fallen—in a *Mer district*? He tried to calculate how long he'd been riding the horse, desperate to put space between himself and the party. Surely it had not been so long.

The horse had done her job well. For him to reach any of the Mer districts would have required a great effort on her part. No wonder he fell off of her in the end. His muscles would punish him later because of the horseback ride.

Peter did not know how to respond. Following Father's death, he'd had no friends or family who visited the Mer for any reason.

Was he welcome? They were treating him kindly while he was injured; would this change when he was able to fight? None of the etiquette he had been taught explained how to behave among Mer.

When he did not react to her words, the woman resumed her work. He allowed himself to stare at her profile while she was busy.

The moneyed used terms such as *fishpeople* when speaking of those who lived in Mer districts. If this woman's claim was true and he was among the Mer, Peter didn't understand such slurs. She didn't look less human than other ladies he knew. She didn't have scales or webbed fingers. Her voice was guarded, but that was to be expected, given the situation.

"You never told me your name," he said. "I hope I did not offend you too much for an introduction."

She had been occupied wiping blood from the side of his head. His question caused her to pause. He saw apprehension, the same hesitance she'd displayed when he first asked.

"You have not offended me, sir." Though she smiled, it was a forced motion. She waited a moment before replying, "My name is—"

The woman broke off, as if someone had tapped her on

the shoulder to prevent a mistake. She resumed the washing of his wound; he noticed that her hand trembled. Her grip had been steady when she began the task.

At last she answered his question.

"My name is…Amelia. My mother owns this orphanage. It's why I was able to get you into the cellar," she added, a bit too hastily. "She has conditions for your stay, but will explain them to you after you've had some sleep."

Peter stared, unconvinced.

Why had it taken her so long to say her name? Why did it feel as if she was hiding something? Perhaps the Mer did not trust him, but he didn't think himself much of a threat, helpless as he was on a cot.

"Thank you, Miss Amelia," he said, disguising his suspicion. "I am grateful."

She looked at him for the first time, and he was struck by the turquoise color of her eyes. Through the fog of pain, he recalled having seen that gaze before, as well as glimpsed her shy smile. It could not be, though—he had never been to the Mer district. Perhaps one of Sybil's friends had a similar face; no other explanation made sense.

He wondered about Amelia's behavior. She had been calm when he woke, but had become tense and jittery. He did not understand her unease; after all, he was not well enough to harm anyone, physically or emotionally.

Amelia spoke again, a tremor in her voice.

"Sir, I hope you can give a valid explanation as to why you are here," she said. "I don't wish to alarm you, but if you cannot account for your presence, you will become the prime suspect for an act of arson committed this night against a local family. It is incredibly bad luck that you should appear now."

Peter grappled with her words. As their gravity set in, the cellar ceased to be a haven. To his tired mind, the walls became thick, closing in to become a prison.

"It wasn't me," he stuttered. "I didn't mean to come here, Miss Amelia. I don't know about the fires, but I promise it wasn't me!"

"I believe you, sir. However, you need to convince Jimmy, the nightwatchman of our street. Tell him the truth. It's easier to remember, and tends to be more convincing."

Peter did not know if *his* truth would be convincing. Would an intelligent nightwatchman believe that he fell off of a horse while fleeing a madwoman? He considered telling the story to Amelia; if she believed him, there was a chance that Jimmy would, as well.

"Get some sleep," Amelia said, standing up and taking the basin. "I'm on your side. You have a trustworthy face."

"What if they don't believe me?" he asked, as she backed towards the stairs. "What will happen then?"

"I don't know," she admitted. "Such a thing has never happened. We are close to the border. If you're feeling well, it's possible you could leave before things escalate."

Her words did not bring him comfort. "Thank you," Peter managed, "for being kind to me."

"It isn't my place to be unkind to anyone," Amelia said, smiling. "I'll leave you to rest. Would you like anything? Milk, tea?"

"No." Peter could not stomach food. He wanted to curl up on the cot and sleep.

"Good night, then," said Amelia. "Don't worry—you aren't alone."

"Thank you."

Peter listened as she walked upstairs and closed the

door. He waited for the click of a lock, but none came. Amelia was telling the truth, then; he was not in prison.

If he felt well enough, he could slip away—but where would he go? He had made such a mess of things that he did not have courage to return home and face the consequences.

What was to become of him?

Four

LADY MEREDITH STOOD NUMB TO THE WHISPERS THAT HAD been triggered by Peter's disappearance. She listened to her father as he spoke to guests behind her.

Lord Bannister had used his cunning to save the night. When Peter's family left in search of him, Bannister used every weapon in his reach. This included lively song, expensive wine, and Meredith's looks.

It did not matter that her intended had disappeared. Meredith was trained to dance with strangers under great pressure. Her heart might have been on the floor in a bloody pile, but she would perform anyway. She only just managed to hold back her tears, made to dance with two ambassadors and a duke.

Wearing her facade was simple on regular days, when she felt nothing. That night, she was dragged through each set like a doll.

Meredith was not given time to gather her wits. She could not slip away to grieve the loss of a future. Instead of offering comfort, Bannister punished her with the shame she already felt.

Most of the guests had left. Meredith found a moment to slip away and sip some wine. Seldom did she drown her sorrows in alcohol, but exceptions existed.

The ball had been a disaster. Both families spent months planning the event, tailoring a perfect guest list, building a spectacle that would grace periodicals.

One thing was for certain: This night would be written about. It would become a hot topic among gossips for the wrong reasons.

Meredith stared at her free hand, watching it tremble as she remembered what she'd done in a moment of terror. Tears continued to sting at her eyes. She would not let them fall in front of the remaining guests. Her emotions would remain hidden until she reached the safety of her bedroom.

I pushed him. Meredith shivered, taking another sip of wine. *Why did I push him?*

Because Peter had become icy. Because he alarmed her with his doubt. Because his words stung when he insisted on a moment alone *to make himself want to marry her.*

Peter had done what no one else could: He had seen through her mask.

Meredith tried to maintain a straight face in his presence, but after one year of flawless acting, she'd lost her nerve.

If she could have found the words to tell Peter what was wrong, would he have believed her? How could she explain to him that Bannister surprised her by inviting the only person she feared?

A person who knew more about her than she dared to

admit. A person who would take her away from all that she knew, because of what she was.

Peter was her only hope of escaping death in life. By making a fool of herself, by hurting him the way she had, Meredith sealed her own fate.

The dreaded person, the guest that she feared, had chosen to stay late. *He* knew that the narrative had turned in his favor. *He* had come to claim his spoils before she could feel a glimmer of hope.

Her heritage meant she had only two prospects suitable for marriage.

From birth, she had never been happy or free, never allowed to dream of love. Yet Meredith tried to rearrange her fate by talking to Peter and his family. Arranged marriages were common among their class, and the Everly-Bannister union would be powerful.

Meredith had been unable to make Peter like her. He went through the motions of proposing to her, but she knew there was no sentiment when he asked Lord Bannister for her hand.

She had hoped to win him over after the wedding, but now knew that there would be no wedding. That was why the other man remained in their ballroom, a cat toying with its food.

Lord Bannister would not give her another opportunity to rearrange her fate. He had taken matters into his own hands the moment he realized Peter had gone.

Meredith remembered the row at the stairs. She was accustomed to using words to get what she wanted. Never before had she committed physical violence against a person. The shame she felt made her want to be sick.

Too much wine. She motioned for a footman to take her glass and wondered if she could excuse herself.

She turned to her father and stiffened. Lord Bannister was talking to *him,* the man she would be married to. No younger than sixty-and-five, he was an eccentric who only wanted her as his wife because...because...

"Mer," whispered Meredith. "I am Mer."

It had always been out of the question for Bannister to admit his daughter had tainted blood. Far be it from him to have a connection with the *fishpeople!* Lady Meredith Bannister's Seasons had been spectacles for the benefit of the titled and wealthy. Her fate had been arranged before she became a woman.

Meredith turned to a portrait of her late mother. Her grief for Countess Bannister had long been overshadowed by rage.

Mother, why couldn't you have been a lady? she asked the woman's serene face.

Countess Adeline Bannister must have known that the Mer-child would have a nightmare of a life. She could have tossed the infant to the sea; perhaps the Merpeople would take her away to a happy place. She could have suffocated the infant with a pillow.

Forced to face the prospect of her future, Meredith wished bitterly that Mother could have suffocated her and ended the suffering early.

"Meredith." Her father's voice was flat. "Come say good-night to Mr. Grumbacher."

No, screamed every fiber of her being as she crossed the ballroom, *no no no no no no no...*

Silas Grumbacher, famous owner of a museum of oddities, was dressed to the nines. She did not like the triumph in his watery eyes as he watched her approach. She felt he was putting a price on her, planning a place for her in his exhibit.

Meredith swallowed, offering Grumbacher a hand. Taking it, he kissed the smooth skin near her wrist; she shuddered when his breath lingered.

"I was just leaving," said Grumbacher, a ghost of his German accent punctuating his words. "It would be ungracious of me to go without saying good-bye."

"Mr. Grumbacher will be paying a call in the morning," said Lord Bannister. With ease he took control of her life, picking up the pieces where she dropped them. "It's late. Get to bed and settle your nerves."

Meredith stared at the ballroom floor, worn from decades of dancing. In her mind, she heard the sound of a cage closing around her.

"Yes, Papa," she choked.

She forced herself to meet Lord Bannister's eyes. They both knew what the call in the morning would be about. Her life would be signed away to the unnerving foreigner.

Peter's late father had been involved with the Mer community. There had been a chance that Peter was not raised with bias against Mer, and Meredith's begging had bought her time to try and win him over. Even Bannister could not argue that a match with the Wests would be favorable for his business.

Meredith lost the gamble when her temper flared on the stairs.

In the morning, she would listen as her father gave her away. In the morning, Grumbacher might put a ring on her finger. In the morning, she would become another interesting object in his collection.

"Good night, Meredith darling," said Lord Bannister.

Perhaps it was the wine, but the way he pronounced the word *darling* made her want to retch.

She wondered at his silence about Peter. Perhaps he would broach the subject when the business with Grumbacher was complete. After he gave her to the nauseous old man, he would reward her with an earful.

"Good night, Papa," Meredith said.

Curtsying to to Grumbacher, she made her exit, wondering where her friends had gone. After the spectacle with Peter, they faded, ghosts in muslin gowns. They were present to witness the scandal, but wouldn't stay to offer support.

Meredith crashed down the corridor to her bedroom. A tear escaped her as she passed the staircase landing. If she had not placed her hands on his chest and pushed—if she had gotten on her knees—if she had groveled, would Peter have stayed?

If she told him why she needed him, would he have made the speech—even if he did not want to?

Meredith slammed her bedroom door, locking it. She stumbled to her bed and grabbed a chamber pot, where she retched all that she had eaten during the feast. The pungent taste of vomit was made worse by the wine.

When her stomach had been emptied of everything except shame, Meredith tore off her gown, throwing it across the room. On her right leg and on her shoulder gleamed patches of pearly white scales. The marks doomed her from infancy; only custom-made gowns had hidden them.

Her maid, Ava, knew of the marks; she was paid a good

wage to keep mum about them. Once Meredith was married away, the maid could not come with her.

"I'll be on a shelf," she whispered, hugging her knees to her chest. "Forgotten, behind glass."

A bitter laugh escaped her. Her scales were precisely the sort of thing that Grumbacher would find interesting.

She wondered if Peter would truly have been more accepting. He had only been a boy when his father advocated for the Merpeople. Meredith could not remember hearing Peter speak of them; they were not on his mind, did not strike his interest. He might have grown up with the bias of the society in which he'd become a man.

Meredith went to her writing desk, reaching for a sheet of paper, and began to pen a letter. Her words were driven by desperation to give form to her agony.

Peter, she wrote.

I know what you must think of me. I know it is futile to say that I am sorry, yet here I am groveling to you on paper.

Peter, I beg that you return one last time. If you would give me a chance to speak, I'll tell you what is to become of me.

You are a better person than I; hear my plea for an audience. I know you would keep my words a secret—although it would not give me escape.

He's coming in the morning...

MEREDITH PAUSED, pen hovering over the page.

She would never send the letter. It would require great audacity on her part to beg a man for help after she nearly killed him. Her palms burned as she remembered the moment she placed them on his chest and shoved.

The pen dropped onto the page.

Hiding her face in her hands, she wept painful and guttural sobs. She had no business writing to Peter. Her fate was sealed; in the morning she would be given to Grumbacher.

It was no more than she deserved.

Meredith took a deep breath. In her crying spell, she'd toppled her bottle of ink; it spilled over the paper, creating a black mark on her desk.

She was marked similarly by the scales on her leg and back. Mother's sin doomed the child that resulted from it.

Mother was dead by her own hand. She fled the world of the living, leaving Meredith to grapple with the aftermath.

Following Mother's death, no one offered kind words. No one knew that Meredith was exhausted from acting. No one asked if she would like to put away her mask.

Meredith existed to please others and do as she was told.

A knock at the door shattered her reverie.

"Miss?" It was Ava. "Do you need help getting out of the corset?"

Meredith stared at the ink on her desk. "Only if you don't ask questions."

Pushing the chair back, she crossed the room and unlocked the door. Ava stood with a gentle smile, holding a tray of tea things. Setting these on a table, she began to sort through Meredith's wardrobe.

"Have all of the guests left?" Meredith asked, staring into the mirror.

What she really wished to ask was *Is Grumbacher gone?*

"All gone, My Lady," said Ava cheerily. "The last carriage set off ten minutes ago. The ballroom is being cleaned; it should be spotless by morning."

Meredith nodded, daring to relax. She would not be comfortable sharing a home with Grumbacher. Regardless, she would be given to him in the morning.

She resolved to enjoy her final hours alone, these moments of relative comfort.

Ava selected a sleeping gown and closed the wardrobe. Meredith saw her glance at the desk with the ink-smudge and waited for questions, but there were none.

Ava did not ask about the desk, the torn dress, or the chamber pot. She focused on helping Meredith out of her corset and into the gown; then, with a promise to have the dress mended by morning, she left Meredith to rest.

Meredith fell asleep to the thought of Grumbacher's hands on her.

In the morning she would be a living experiment to poked and prodded. She no longer had the right to protest.

If ever she'd had a future with Peter, her act of impulse ended it.

She would go with Grumbacher, for she had no weapons left. She would go, because her soul was marked by her attempted sin.

She drifted off to the image of Peter falling down the stairs, knowing it would haunt her for the rest of her life.

Five

Amelia's voice woke Peter from a restless slumber: "Sir, Jimmy has come by for a visit. He wishes to speak with you."

Sleep had been no refuge for Peter; it brought to him dreams which were filled with the sensation of falling. He remembered the helplessness he felt when tumbling backwards.

It was a never-ending fall, and he had no respite from his fear. He fell and fell and fell...

"Jimmy?" he repeated.

"The watchman who helped bring you downstairs."

With a jolt, Peter remembered the events of the previous night. He was suspect in an act of arson that he knew nothing about. The watchman was going to come and talk; his freedom depended on his telling the truth, and whether this watchman would believe him.

Dread settled in the pit of his stomach. How could he have had such bad luck? Was it not enough that he couldn't go home, that his reputation was in shambles? Now he needed to say the right words in order to clear his name.

"Did you sleep well?" Amelia asked, lightening her tone; perhaps she saw the dread in his face. "How are you feeling?"

Peter sat up. Aside from a dull throb on the side of his head, he was rested enough. There was no amnesia—he remembered well enough the things he wished to forget—and none of his bones were broken. In place of being crippled from the fall, he was wrought with anxiety.

Anything could come from that interview with the watchman.

"I slept," he replied, "and I am feeling better. Thank you for helping me."

Amelia nodded. "I'm glad to hear that. Do you think you are well enough to meet with Jimmy? He's upstairs, but I could tell him you're still in recovery. He would understand."

"I would rather have it done now," Peter said warily. "It doesn't matter if I tell him another day; he might yet disbelieve me."

"He is a kind man," Amelia assured him. "So long as he senses you are telling the truth, I don't think the conversation can go wrong."

"Perhaps." Peter shrugged. "I've only had bad luck for months, and there's no reason why that should change."

"Tell the truth," Amelia advised. "It has a weight of its own. I will send him down and bring a tray of breakfast."

Peter found himself distracted by her smile. Not only was it lovely—it demanded to be looked at, light and pure—but it was familiar. He had seen this woman before, had seen such a smile with dimples and blue eyes, but the fog in his mind was so great that it prevented him access to his oldest memories.

Perhaps he did suffer from memory loss.

"Thank you, Miss Amelia," he said, also smiling—beautiful smiles should be returned. "Could you stay while he's here? I don't fancy being interrogated alone."

"Certainly. I'll be back."

Amelia curtsied, a startlingly perfect dip of the knee, the sort that was taught to children when young and written so deeply into their bodies that time and space could not erase them.

Amelia could not have been born in a Mer district. Traces of a gentle upbringing were present in all that she did.

She hurried upstairs once more and vanished behind the door.

Peter stood, leaning on the wall for a moment, but felt no dizziness. He smoothed his hair into something acceptable, wishing he had asked to borrow a comb. Briefly he thought of donning his jacket, which had been hung on a nail on the wall, but it was in tatters.

A male voice spoke from behind the door. "...excellent, Mrs. Whittle, thank you. I won't be long. No, no worries, I only have some questions."

Peter cleared his throat, straightened his posture to wait.

Amelia emerged again, carrying a tray of breakfast things, coffee and sandwiches of some sort. The man from the night before followed her. Peter remembered his face vaguely, but stepped forward for a better look.

He was a man of respectable bearing, silver streaks in light brown hair, lines on his face denoting a life well lived. Peter was relieved that Jimmy did not have an unkind expression. He looked at the wounded guest with concern, not loathing. It might be easy to speak with him, after all.

"Good morning," Jimmy said to Peter as he descended. "It's a relief to see you up on your own."

"Thank you, sir."

Peter reached up and took the tray from Amelia; with a smile, she finished her descent. She looked at him, her eyes saying that he should relax.

He gave a slight nod, setting the tray on a crate. The cellar must have doubled as storage, for wooden boxes were scattered about. They served as seats for the three of them, who settled in a wide circle to face each other.

"I hear you're feeling better," said Jimmy the watchman. "That's good. You took quite a bad fall."

"I did," Peter agreed. "Thank you for helping me walk. I was rather shocked when you discovered me."

"Understandable," said Jimmy. "Now I have some inquiries regarding why you were here. Please take no offense—it's only that our visitors are so rare, we can't help but feel suspicion at a sudden appearance."

Peter nodded. He glanced at Amelia, who focused on pouring coffee into three cups. She had a serene look on her face; if she was not worried by this conversation, he would also relax.

"Ask away," said Peter, hoping his voice did not sound worried. Why should he have been worried? After all, he knew in his heart that he had not committed arson.

"Very good." The watchman shrugged and said, "My first question is simple. Who are you?"

Peter accepted his cup from Amelia and stirred, a desperate attempt to buy time.

Amelia told him to be honest, that the truth itself held

weight. He wished to remain anonymous, did not want to reveal himself as Lord Everly. Despite the circumstances, he found in the cellar much-needed respite from the title he inherited.

They would know if he lied, though. He had no choice but to bear the burden again.

"I am Lord Peter West," he said slowly, not looking away from his coffee. "I recently inherited earldom over the Everly property. I am here because I made some bad choices and fled. Unfortunately I did not know where I was headed, and wound up on Miss Amelia's lawn."

His title had the expected effect. Jimmy stared with great surprise; Amelia kept her eyes fixed on the ground, something like sadness in her expression.

"You are the son of Lord David West?" Jimmy asked, breathless. "Well, that changes everything. He remains a hero among our people, though no one has heard from him in years."

"He has died," Peter said. He repeated those words so often during sleepless nights that he was able to say them without breaking down. "I am glad to hear he is remembered well."

"Oh, indeed he is," said Jimmy, and it was he who struggled to speak now, grief darkening his tone. "He was a friend to many of us, a valued connection with the outside world, and a man with great sympathy for the Merpoeple."

Amelia continued to stare at the ground. Her silence made Peter uneasy. He had wished for her presence so the conversation would not be stifling; instead he seemed to have angered her.

Jimmy cleared his throat of emotion. "I am deeply sorry

to hear that your father died. We did wonder why his visits ceased."

"He chose to focus on his family after Lord Finch's death. I don't think he forgot this place, but it would have been painful for him to continue visiting."

"I understand." Jimmy hesitated. "That doesn't explain, though—how did you arrive here?"

Peter smiled with no cheer. "I'm afraid it is no hero's tale. I had a row and cannot go home yet. I mounted a horse and took off, but had no heading in mind. At some point I fell off of the horse, and you know the rest. It truly is that embarrassing."

Jimmy raised his eyebrows. "What could you have done that is bad enough to prevent you from going home?"

The truth bears weight, Amelia said.

He did not want to say the truth of it, but if she believed it might be helpful, he would try.

"I refused to marry the woman my mother picked for me," he said, "and did so in a manner that will reflect badly on everyone."

Could his ridiculous truth be enough to convince the watchman?

Peter hadn't entered their community to commit arson. He was there because he'd been a fool, mounting a horse while bleary from falling down stairs. He could not even be sure of how long he'd been riding before unconsciousness gripped him.

Jimmy did not respond. He studied Peter's face in the manner some people did when scouring for honesty.

Peter watched for evidence that he was being ridiculed, but found none. There was pity, which could not be entirely bad–if Jimmy felt pity for him, it must mean he believed some of the story.

"I know that you're concealing part of your motive," said the watchman, "and I don't blame you. In your situation, I would not want to say it all, either. I don't believe you're responsible for the fire, because when we found you last night, you did not smell of smoke. I also don't believe you are responsible, because your father was kind to us. I wish you had arrived under better circumstances."

Amelia exhaled with relief. Peter also felt it, too; sweet release crept through his exhaustion.

"Thank you," he managed. "Is there anything I can do to help?"

Jimmy straightened and said, "It depends on how committed you wish to be. I won't burden you with entreaties. I invite you to stay while you recover."

Peter was grateful for the invitation. He did not feel brave enough to make the journey home; he didn't even know how far *home* was.

"Will Mrs. Whittle agree to let him stay?" Jimmy asked Amelia, who at last had looked up.

"I don't think she would take issue," Amelia replied. "Have a word with her. She might appreciate your reassurances."

Jimmy nodded, rising. "I'll get that done, then," he said, placing his unfinished coffee on the crate where he'd been sitting.

Turning to Peter, he added, "We will be discreet about your presence while you recover. Would you like me to find you something comfortable to wear? I must say, that suit has seen better days."

"I would be grateful," Peter said.

"Then I'll be back tonight. Thank you for the coffee, Miss Ro—er, Miss Amelia."

Peter looked up, puzzled at Jimmy's slip of tongue. He said nothing, though his suspicion deepened that something was being hidden from him.

"Are you attending the funeral?" Jimmy asked Amelia, who nodded.

"We leave in less than an hour," she said. "And you?"

"I'll be organizing it. I hear the mother is inconsolable." Jimmy shook his head. "I'd best head off. They'll have started to gather."

"Thank you, Jimmy," Amelia said. "I'll walk you out."

Peter said nothing as they left, sipping his coffee in the solitude of the cellar. Why was he being lied to? If he had told the truth about his identity, was it fair that she should fool him with an alias?

Amelia was not gone long. She returned with that same pretty smile, but something in her eyes was troubled. "I'm afraid I will be gone for a few hours," she said, clasping her hands. "As you might have overheard, there is a funeral. A baby died in that fire. When one of our people dies, we all grieve."

She offered him a plate with bread rolls.

He accepted it and asked, "A child was killed? Why aren't we hearing of such incidents at home?"

Amelia turned away. "Because your lot would prefer it if we did not exist. Do you think a journalist would mar his newspaper with the mention of these districts?" She shook her head. "They don't care, and they don't want you to care. That is why you don't know about these crimes, and why they go unpunished."

"That isn't right," Peter said, staring at the roll. "I did not study for so long to remain ignorant of such an important, unjust matter. How long has this been happening, Miss Amelia?"

He spoke the name casually, not wanting her to know of his suspicions yet.

"For as long as I have been here," she said, and their eyes locked.

The color of her eyes, like that precious turquoise stone, was bolder in the sunlight. Peter *knew* he had seen this young woman before, and his gut told him strongly that her name was not Amelia.

He saw in her a timidity, though, which caused him to refrain from asking questions.

Instead he said, "I want to go to the funeral."

Those eyes—so bold, so lovely—widened. "To the funeral?"

"Is there a law stating I cannot attend?" he challenged.

Amelia shook her head, dumbfounded. "Do you think it wise to leave so soon after your injury?"

Peter fixed his eyes on the window above. "I won't be happy in a cellar, sitting in the ignorance imposed on me. I want to see your district, Miss Amelia. Unless there is a law saying I cannot attend, I would like to go to the funeral."

"There is no law," she stammered. "You see, sir—er, Lord Everly—our funerals are at the beach. The bodies of our departed are given to the Merpeople in the ocean. They dispose of the remains as they see fit."

"You don't believe I can walk to the beach," Peter guessed. "Is it far?"

"No," she said, after a pause. "There is a decent view from here. This orphanage is not far from the beach. Mrs.

Whittle would prefer it if the girls did not know you're here. We would have to let them go first."

"Mrs. Whittle, your mother?" he could not help asking, a challenge.

Amelia stiffened. "Yes. My mother."

"You aren't a good liar," Peter heard himself say, "whoever you are."

Her cheeks had become slightly pink; she made a show of tidying the silverware on the breakfast tray. "Yes, well," she said in a huff, "neither are you, *Lord Peter West.*"

Peter knew he had made her angry because she was leaning away from him again.

"Who are you?" he whispered. "Why are you hiding your identity from me? I have told the truth about who I am."

Clang. She dropped a spoon on an empty plate.

"As if your family cared for my identity," she said hotly, "when my mother and I were driven away!"

"I don't understand," he said—her anger was palpable and made him want to become very small. "Have I done something to harm you?"

"No," she said, her words clipped. "Not you in specific."

"Then why punish me?"

"Because she died!" the young woman cried, shoving the tray, a display of anger far from the gentle lady he met the night before. "Lady Rose *died* when your father *forgot* about her. You are looking at what remains of her, but she is not what you knew. Do not pretend you know me," she finished, and he was grieved to see a tear slide down her face. "My features are the same but I am a different person. Perhaps I could not have carried out my lie much longer—they call me an open book. Do not pretend that you know me, *Lord Peter West,* for Lady Rose no longer exists."

"Lady Rose," he whispered, her words swimming around him like a school of drunken fish. "Everyone assumed..."

"That I had died, yes?" she asked, grabbing the tray. "It isn't far from the truth. I died the day my mother and I came *here* to find shelter. We were welcomed by Mrs. Whittle because of Mother's heritage. When *my mother* died," she added, voice breaking, "she was also given to the sea. Lady Rose is dead, *Lord Peter West,* so you might well go on calling me Amelia. I will tell Mrs. Whittle you want to attend the funeral. Something will be arranged."

"Lady Rose," he called as she turned to the stairs. "I didn't mean to make you angry. I was told you were dead. If I had known..."

"Don't call me *Lady Rose!* If you had known, then what?" she demanded. "Would you have gotten on your mighty black horse and come to the rescue? Fate has placed our cards as such, and you are still rich, while I have become the bane of your existence. Perhaps you won't want me to treat you anymore. I can call for a *human* doctor to finish tending your wound."

"Rose!" he said again as she hurried up the stairs, but she vanished without another word.

Sighing, he stared at the roll of bread that he had not yet eaten. It was stale, but he would not be so rude as to point it out. He tore it into small pieces, soaked it in his coffee, and waited for the world to be right again.

Lady Rose had been Sybil's friend. When Peter and Sybil were young, Rose would join them as they explored the estate owned by the Wests. They spent hours skipping rocks, collecting feathers, and racing. In the spring they would gather wildflowers, identifying them using the books in Father's library.

Those had been delightful years. Peter hadn't yet known of the responsibility that awaited him as a firstborn male. No one could have told him he would face these responsibilities so early in life.

He closed his eyes, but found that shock had quite woken him up. Though he lacked an appetite, he finished the bread.

There was a stretch in which he wondered whether Rose would reappear; her serenity had shattered with the unveiling of her identity. At long last, however, Rose returned, her eyes red and puffy.

Peter felt a stab of guilt. He hadn't wanted to make her cry; he only wanted the truth!

"Mrs. Whittle says you may attend the funeral with me," she said, directing her words to the floor rather than at him. "She is leaving with the girls; we can follow in ten minutes."

Peter nodded. "Tell me if there is some protocol I must follow." Hastily he added, "Please."

Rose stared at her clasped hands and giggled. The sound gave him hope that she would not be angry forever.

"Don't wear those cufflinks," she advised. "You and I will watch from a distance. I would advise you to dress as a street urchin, but your clothes are already in that state."

He smiled; how else could he react to such an amusing truth? "Thank you," he said.

Rose waved his thanks away and offered him a hand. He hesitated before accepting, though he tried to do most of the work so she would not carry the weight of him. She had become so thin…

Peter felt an urge to kiss her hand, the way he would have if things had been better—if her father had not died— if she had not renounced the title given to her at birth.

In a better world, they would have danced at a ball. They would have played croquet at a garden party. He would have seen her become a woman, rather than being told she had vanished.

Before he could give in to that urge, she reached for his coat.

"It's dirty enough," she said, smiling. In that smile, he saw the young girl who had once helped him gather daisies.

"Not dirty enough," Peter said. He grabbed one of the sleeves and tore until there was a large, unsightly gap. "There. Now I shall look like a street urchin."

Rose stared at the damage he had done to his tailored coat. She shook her head, smirking with genuine mirth.

"No," she said, "you will never look like a street urchin."

Peter worked at removing the cufflinks from his clothing, tucking them into the pillowcase, and wondered whether her words had been a compliment.

You will never look like a street urchin.

Six

ROSE AND PETER LISTENED TO A CACOPHONY OF VOICES upstairs. These consisted of eight orphans and a woman who sounded brusque and intolerant.

Rose resisted the smile that tugged at her face upon seeing Peter's expression.

"In a line, in a line!" Mrs. Whittle called. "Lower your voices, this is a funeral. Shortest to tallest—Anne, you stand there—Marie, you're the tallest, by the door. Holding hands, holding hands, we don't want to lose any of you."

A young girl's voice piped in; she spoke too softly to make out her words.

"Miss Rose is on an errand," Mrs. Whittle said, "and Marie is standing in for her." A pause, another voice. "Yes, Marie. You are." Another pause. "Because I have decided. I can change my mind whenever I want to, Marie, you know that well. Lead the girls to the shore. I have to grab something downstairs to offer the Hardys. An offering of sympathy. *Go!*"

There was a scuffle of footsteps as the girls ran out the door. Rose grinned, imagining them tripping over one another in their rush to get away.

Then came the sound of Mrs. Whittle's footsteps as she neared the cellar door. Peter looked at Rose with alarm and whispered, "Does she bite?"

Rose muffled her giggle with a hand, but did not provide him with an answer. She had the rather unkind desire to see how this man-from-the-*ton* would react to Mrs. Whittle's welcome.

"Should I get on the cot?" he asked, turning a shade pale.

Creak, said the door as Mrs. Whittle opened it and made her way into the cellar.

"Is he awake?" she called, making her steady descent.

"Yes, ma'am," Rose said, struggling to keep a straight face. Mrs. Whittle didn't like to be laughed at. "Standing and everything."

"Good, good." Mrs. Whittle stopped at the foot of the stairs, eyeing the gentleman in the corner. "Amelia has told me that she is Rose again, so I won't have to participate in that ridiculous charade. She says you remember your name."

"Er," said the man, "yes. I do."

"Let's hear it, then," said Mrs. Whittle.

Peter glanced at Rose. She heard the unspoken question: *Do I need to use my title?*

Rose shrugged. Jimmy might have told Mrs. Whittle that Peter was Lord David West's son; hiding his identity could be futile. Even if he managed to conceal his title, his fine clothes and purebred horse were telling.

Peter inhaled a breath. "My name—" He broke off, swallowing. "I am Lord Peter West, Earl of Everly."

Rose shook her head with sadness. When Peter introduced himself earlier, she had known that he could not be Earl of Everly unless his father had died. Perhaps it should have occurred to her when she noticed him wearing the signet ring that he was more than the earl's son. Now she wondered whether she ought to curtsy to him in greeting.

Mrs. Whittle did not bat an eye at Peter's use of his title, and she certainly did not curtsy.

"I don't botch my words, Lord Everly," she said; Rose watched Peter's puzzlement increase. "My girls are starving. They haven't had full bellies for a week. You are welcome to spend as much time in our cellar as you need, but I am here for some form of payment so that I can feed them."

Rose battled an urge to stop Mrs. Whittle from confronting her patient about money, but the woman was right. The bread Rose acquired the night before was gone. She hoped that Peter had a good heart, for she wanted the children in her care to have a meal.

Peter crossed the room to the cot; reaching into the pillowcase, he retrieved the gold cufflinks Jimmy had been eyeing.

"I do not have currency on me," he said, "but heaven knows I don't need these. Sell them. I'm sure they will provide many meals."

Mrs. Whittle eyed the cufflinks with her equivalent of shock—an eye twitch accompanied by a sniff. "Surely you only mean to give me one."

"No," he said. "Take them both. I was going to ask how long you would allow me to stay, Mrs. Whittle." He spoke the woman's name with respect, as if addressing a debutante. "You see, I—I'm not ready to go home. In more ways than one, I confess that respite in your cellar could do me well. If you will have me, of course. These cufflinks will feed the children. I only ask that you set aside enough to pay whoever is caring for my horse."

Mrs. Whittle glanced at Rose, whose heart ached as she listened to Peter's words.

When he forced her to reveal her identity, she'd gone upstairs to settle her temper. How dare a West *make* her do anything after they had abandoned her during the most crucial years of her life?

Peter's eyes shone with grief. She knew he was not like the others of his society. He would never make coarse jokes about the Mer at a dinner table.

He was in pain, but not because of his injury. Something inside of him had been broken, and he sought healing in a place no person would voluntarily enter.

Mrs. Whittle sniffed again before snatching the cufflinks out of his hand.

"You can stay for as long as you need," she said, pocketing them. "Rose, bring him upstairs for dinner tonight. I'll sell these and have Cook buy what's needed for something hearty." She looked once more at Peter, adding with a touch of kindness, "If you intend to stay, I will have a room and bath prepared when you return. One day you will have children, and you'll understand the urgency to have them fed."

"I understand now," he said, voice cracking for some reason. "Thank you. A bath would be nice. I smell of horse."

"I'm leaving now. Rose will take you someplace you can see the pier without being noticed."

Mrs. Whittle shot Rose a look that she could not interpret, but there was something of amusement in it. She then turned and ascended the stairs, two steps at a time, *singing* under her breath. Mrs. Whittle never sang! She must have been in a good mood indeed.

Neither of them spoke until they heard the front door open and close, indicating Mrs. Whittle's departure.

Rose turned to Peter, who had not moved from his spot at the center of the room. "Let's go, then," she said. "Unless you aren't feeling well."

"I feel better here," he whispered, "than I've felt at home in a long time." Offering a shaky smile, he looked at her hand and hesitated before taking it, a quick gesture of peace.

"Can you walk?"

"I can walk," he said.

They ascended the stairs, stepping onto the ground floor. Peter looked at everything, from the paintings on the wall to the cuckoo clock. Evidence abounded that this was a female residence: dolls, bits of fabric, and buttons were scattered on chairs, all of which were covered by mismatched doilies.

"This is cozy," he said.

"It belonged to Mr. Whittle," Rose explained as they headed for the door. "When they married, it was their home. Unfortunately, their marriage did not last. He was killed less than a year later."

"Killed?" Peter repeated.

Rose allowed him to step first into the warm sunlight. He inched out, looking in all directions, as if expecting the grass to be red or some other such nonsense.

"A man killed him," she said, locking the door, "because he was given the job they competed for. God forbid that anyone from the Mer district should make a living as a

69

blacksmith. The man who killed him wasn't punished, but was offered the position as a replacement."

Peter stared, eyes gleaming with anger. "Not punished?" he cried.

"Mrs. Whittle kept the house," Rose continued, "but she lost her baby." Lowering her gaze, she finished, "The baby was called Amelia. It's why I used her name. Amelia was given to the sea in a ceremony like the one you are going to witness."

She locked the door with a key she wore on a chain around her neck.

Turning, she found Peter once more staring at the buildings surrounding him. She wondered if he would use the word *cozy* to describe the streets of this district.

The sidewalks were narrow, buildings disheveled. Mrs. Whittle's orphanage was the best looking on their block, because the orphans who married would have their husbands help with maintenance. Across the street stood a line of houses built of rotting wood. Some had boarded windows, a bid for safety against the nightly attacks.

"Where is my horse?" Peter asked, as they walked around the orphanage.

"The Moores' home is there," Rose said, pointing to a house next door. "You can't see it, but they have a stable in the back. Your horse will be safe with them."

"Yes," Peter said softly.

They stepped through the hedges onto the cliff that overlooked the ocean where Merpeople lived. He paused; she knew he was overcome by the beauty of the sight before him. It was said that nowhere else was the ocean so blue.

"Yes," he said again. "I know she is safe."

She smiled. "Let's be going, then."

He glanced at her and nodded.

"Beautiful," she heard him whisper, as they walked down the beaten path.

Rose wondered what it was he had called beautiful.

Certainly the ocean. It had to be that.

Seven

"Would you like to wear the blue gown, My Lady?" Ava asked.

Meredith had always wondered when her maid slept. The sun had scarcely begun to rise before Ava swept in to wake her. Lord Bannister must have given her orders that Meredith should be presentable in time for Grumbacher's visit.

When she did not reply at once, Ava added, "It's new, My Lady, and you haven't tried it on in public. If you would prefer something else, that would also do."

"I don't care," Meredith said, unable to find the strength to move a limb. "Yes. The blue. Might as well use it."

At least the blue dress was not stained or torn up. She cringed, remembering the fate of her gown the night before.

"The bath is ready for you." Ava took the blue dress from Meredith's wardrobe. She was a terrific actress, speaking as if she had not witnessed her mistress in a drunken stupor hours before. "A tray of breakfast is being brought up."

Meredith glanced at the timepiece beside her bed. It was

seven-thirty. Her time of freedom had ended the moment Peter vanished.

She chose to pretend that in these final minutes—while she was in the bath, before the guest arrived—there were not yet chains binding her.

If only it were so simple.

"Thank you, Ava," she whispered, sitting up.

Meredith's hands trembled; she found them repulsive. She could not forget the sight of them shoving Peter to his possible death, injuring the only person who could have helped her.

It was pointless to devise another way out. She had been playing a game of chess throughout her courtship with Peter. She'd known all along that, if she did not win, Bannister would proceed with his arrangement.

In the end, Meredith lost the game.

Marriage to Grumbacher was an appropriate punishment for attempted murder.

SHE ALLOWED HERSELF A LONG BATH. With fragrant soap she scrubbed at her skin, wishing to feel clean of her sickness the night before. She took care when washing the scales on her leg. If not treated gently, the marks caused days of pain.

She had once attempted to remove a scale by force, not waiting for it to fall. The ensuing pain began someplace deep inside of her, more secret than those that made her a woman. Years later, she did not know the nature of that hidden place, but the memory of that pain cautioned her not to mistreat the scales.

Meredith only needed to face the monstrosity of her

origin when bathing. Ava would dress her to perfection, and no one would guess that ocean-blood ran through her veins.

Staring at the scales, Meredith sighed. They had grown, spreading as she aged. She wondered if, by the end of her life, the mark would claim her entire body. Would she have no way to hide the truth as an old woman? Who would want to bury the likes of her in their cemetery?

Death.

Meredith flung the sponge away, wringing water out of her hair. Life with Grumbacher would be death. She did not know his intentions with her, only that he wanted her because of her origin.

What was more disgusting to think of, sharing his bed, or being in his cage?

After the bath, Ava helped Meredith into a striking blue day dress and wound her hair in a knot. Meredith chose to wear a pearl necklace that had belonged to her mother. She felt no love for her mother's memory, but the weight of the pearls comforted her. They reminded her that she had been born from somebody.

She then thanked Ava and left the room, bracing herself for the end.

Lord Bannister did not waste precious seconds telling her *good morning,* occupied with a newspaper. Meredith did not take offense at his silence. It meant she did not need to feign pleasant talk.

"Am I to act surprised?" she asked, sitting across from him at the table.

"I don't care how you act," he said, "so long as you don't break from the plan."

The plan. "Am I going to be his wife, or his experiment?"

"I did not ask."

Meredith felt a dizzy spell and closed her eyes. Despite all the lessons she had taken, dances she learned, and languages she spoke, she remained unimportant to the man before her. If she died, he would not care.

A servant approached with a glass of water, placing it before her. She knew it contained a high volume of sea salt. From birth, she had needed salt water for strength. It was one of many characteristics that made her abominable. She wondered how Grumbacher would use it to his advantage.

As she drank, Lord Bannister lowered his newspaper. He glanced at the timepiece and said, "Any moment now."

She had never seen such glee on his face. At last he would be rid of the monster his wife created with one of the *fishpeople*. He would be free to marry again, if he so wished, without the need to explain his daughter's repulsive habits. He would continue his life as if Meredith never existed.

"We will wait in the parlor," Lord Bannister decided, getting to his feet and striding off.

Meredith finished her water and followed, managing to keep her head up despite her low spirits. She sat on an armchair by the window and grabbed a book from a table nearby, pretending to read.

Staring at the words on the page, she wondered what had become of Peter. Did he find help after she assaulted him? Was he alive? She had not heard from his mother or sister, so his fate remained a mystery.

Lord Bannister instructed the butler that Mr. Grumbacher should be shown into the parlor. The old man was coming directly to claim his goods. There would be no stalling with tea or small talk.

Meredith remembered the day that Grumbacher learned

about Peter, Lord Everly's visits. When told of the possibility that Peter would propose, there had been no rage on Grumbacher's part. Instead, he smiled and sipped his wine, a knowing look on his face. A man of business, Grumbacher might have been aware that the cards were stacked against her.

Even as Meredith pondered this, Silas Grumbacher's arrival was announced by the butler. She shut the book and rose to greet him, determined to meet her future head-on. Her hands trembled as she listened to Bannister and Grumbacher exchange words in the entrance. Why the delay? Could they not hasten and be done with it?

Lord Bannister did not enter the room with Grumbacher, which brought her surprise. She would have expected him to see the proposal through until the end, ensuring that she did not dishonor him. That was not the case, however; it appeared that he had wiped his hands clean of her.

Grumbacher wore gems of different colors on his wrinkled fingers. She hated looking at his hands, remembering the day he touched her leg.

Mother had not been dead for a week when Lord Bannister found someone to relieve him of Meredith. She remembered the ride to Grumbacher's home, a building hidden on a vast green plain. She remembered Grumbacher asking for proof that she had Mer blood. The proof had been on her leg, a patch of scales that would bring her shame for the rest of her life.

Had it not been enough that day for Grumbacher to see the scales? What had been the need to touch them, when she was only a child? Years later, she could not forget the nauseous sensation.

Grumbacher would now be able to touch her whenever he wished to.

The full exposure of the sunlight made him look older. He took off his hat and began his approach, leaning on his cane. She hated that cane. She wanted to toss it into the fire.

"Well, well," he said, setting his hat on a footstool. "Here we are at last."

She felt a shiver but managed a steady voice when she said, "Yes. Here we are."

"He slipped the hook," said Silas Grumbacher, and she did flinch at the reminder of Peter.

More like I shoved him back into the sea, Meredith thought.

"For heavens' sake, get it over with," she blurted out. "Or are you too old to get down on one knee?"

"Even if I could," he said, giving her the look of disgust to which she was accustomed, "I would not. You know why I am here, Daughter of the Sea."

Meredith did not realize she was crying until he produced from his pocket a box. He opened it to reveal the largest diamond she had ever seen. Her tears soon blurred its shiny surface; her chest constricted with sobs she managed to suppress.

He did not ask the dreaded question, sparing her the need to answer it. Accepting her silence as defeat, he took the ring and slipped it on her finger.

It is heavy, she thought, unused to such weight in jewelry.

Looking over Silas' shoulder, she saw Lord Bannister watching triumphantly.

"When," she whispered, "am I to be given away, then?"

Eight

ROSE KNEW OF A PLACE WHERE SHE AND PETER COULD WATCH the funeral. Having been warned by Jimmy that they ought to avoid being seen, she chose a location where once she had found shelter from the world.

One evening, shortly after arriving with her mother, Rose had slipped away from the orphanage in search of a place of solitude. Her keen eyes soon found a trail; it wound off the beaten sidewalk to a firm precipice. The precipice offered a breathtaking view of the ocean and shore; there she had spent many evenings, swallowing away her tears.

After Mother's death, Mrs. Whittle had hired Rose as a teacher. She stopped visiting the precipice, fearing that one of her pupils might find it and fall. As her new life became focused on teaching, the place slipped from her mind.

Peter's request to see the ceremony gave it a new purpose.

"Where are we going?" Peter asked.

Rose glanced at him, concerned that the exercise might

prove too much for his injuries. The young man showed no signs of fatigue, his gait determined and steady.

"To an old refuge of mine," she said.

"Refuge?"

Rose decided there was no harm in telling the story.

"When Mother and I first came, I wanted nothing to do with the place. I was a child and missed my house. I longed for the life I had known before."

Her voice became wistful as she remembered the most vulnerable years of her life.

"Years passed before I was able to accept that my home was an orphanage. I hated the different customs of the Merpeople; I hated that this place was forsaken by constables. On days when homesickness became too heavy, I craved solitude. Seeking it, I found a path."

They stopped before a cluster of large rocks. They concealed had an opening large enough for a person to slip through with little effort. She motioned for Peter to come near it.

"If you can fit through that opening," she said, "and mind the shallow steps, you will find my hiding place. It offers a grand view of the ocean."

Peter peered into the rocks; she saw in his expression a glimpse of the boy she had once known. In their days of innocent play, young Peter used to squeeze through small paths, simply to prove that he could.

"The steps won't collapse?" he asked.

"No," said Rose. "I would have fallen long ago. The real question is, are you physically able? It's a bit narrow."

"I have ventured this far from home without dying," Peter said. "I'm not afraid of a rocky trail. But must *ladies first* apply here? If one of us must free-fall…"

Rose laughed at his hesitance. "I assure you, I'm not in danger. Pay attention when I climb down—you'll get an idea of where to step. It's important to watch your footing, as some steps are uneven."

With that, she squeezed into the passage, inching towards the precipice. She heard Peter follow a moment later with surprising stealth; the fall from the steed must not have affected him after all.

Once she had emerged on the precipice, Rose offered Peter a hand, afraid he might lose his balance. Though he accepted the help, he showed no signs of fatigue. Together, they sat on the rough, sandy ground to wait.

"I should have thought to bring a blanket," Rose said, noting the roughness of the ground.

Peter did not reply. His eyes were drawn to the people gathered on the beach, near the foaming waves. One might expect to hear conversation from such a crowd, but the descendants of Merpeople kept silence on such solemn occasions.

Grief wafted up to the precipice where Rose and Peter hid. As they breathed it in, they lost the desire for banter. Grief was a fog that blurred trivial emotions; only a person with no heart would be unaffected by the death of a baby.

She lost track of the minutes that passed as more people joined the mourners below. When at last song filled the air, it stirred her from a dream.

Rose had heard the mourning song before, a melody was said to have come from the Sirens, the wildest of Merpeople. It was a forever lullaby, a song of thanks for the life of the deceased person.

The sound brought her a bitter memory. With this melody, her mother had been given to the ocean. Rose first heard the funeral dirge on the day she became alone in the world.

Hugging her knees to her chest, Rose fought the recollection. She wanted to appear strong while showing Peter her home, but could not bring herself to see the disposal of the casket.

She huddled against the cliff, concentrating on breathing in and out.

Peter watched, eyebrows knit with fascination. Rose's shoulders relaxed as she watched him, endeared by his curiosity. He must have been the only person since his father to take an interest in the customs of Mer.

The song became softer as voices dropped. Rose knew that the casket was now near the waves, where Mermen prepared to take it away.

She had never been able to stomach the fleeting nature of Mer funerals. Giving a casket to the sea brought less closure than burying it in the ground.

AT MOTHER'S FUNERAL, Rose had been forced to stand at the front, watching pallbearers carry Mother's casket to the water. Panic broke through her grief when she glimpsed the Mermen waiting to receive the casket.

"No," she had said. "Not in the ocean!"

Mrs. Whittle held her in place and said, "It's what she wanted, dear. To be with her father, her people."

"Bury her in the ground!" Rose begged. "Somewhere I can visit her! Bury her next to Pappa!"

"How do you propose we do that?" Mrs. Whittle asked.

"Do you think those people would want her body in their ground? You know how we are seen by them. They would desecrate your mother's remains."

"Change her name," Rose cried. "Bury her in your yard! Don't take her away from me!"

"She's in your heart, child," Mrs. Whittle said.

Rose had dissolved into her misery, watching Mother's casket disappear beneath the waves. She would have no place where she could leave Mother a flower.

The casket disappeared, sealing in her mind the crushing loneliness of her life. That day, she became a proper orphan.

"WHO TOOK THE CASKET?" Peter asked. "It was made of wood—it ought to have floated!"

"Mermen are strong," said Rose. "They alone know where our dead are taken. Perhaps there's a cave where remains are left to become one with the sea."

In her distraction, Rose hadn't noticed him moving to the edge of the precipice, seeking a better view.

"I did not see any Mermen," he said with disappointment.

"If you stay long enough," Rose said, "perhaps you will."

Peter turned to her, and she was taken aback by how the sun enhanced his features. The boy had grown into a handsome man with hair of gold and eyes like the ocean. More beautiful than their color was the wonder in them.

"Rose?" he asked sheepishly.

She could not resist the smile that tugged at her lips. "Yes?"

"I—I would like to collect seashells," Peter said. Rose chuckled, for he was blushing as he spoke his request. "If you would only tell me the way down, I'll go—"

"Don't be silly, Peter," she said, surprised that she could use his Christian name when they had been apart for so long. "Of course I'm going with you. I can't let you take all the good shells, can I?"

She thought she saw his lip tremble, but he gathered himself quickly. "What's the prize if I collect more?"

Rose pondered this for a stretch before deciding. "Whoever wins is allowed to ask any question to an honest answer."

"*Any* question?"

"Any question. We've both been hiding things, and I think it's time for honesty."

Peter nodded with some bewilderment. Getting to his feet, he offered her a hand and helped her up off the ground. Rose fixed her gaze on her feet, not wanting to stare at him so openly.

"Your terms are fair enough," Peter said. "Though you could ask me anything and I would tell you now."

"What would be the fun in that?" Rose shook her head, smiling. "Follow me—I know a quick way to the sand."

Rose stepped away from the precipice, not releasing his hand. She wondered at the possessiveness that had taken hold of her. Perhaps it was due to the fact that Peter was a figure from her past. There was nothing she would rather do than play a game with him of collecting seashells.

There was freedom in being childish with the person she had known as a child. However, it did not mean she would let him win.

Rose began to think of a question to ask if she should emerge the victor. As they neared the water, it struck her.

Why did you run away? she would ask. *What's gone so wrong that you would forsake your life of comfort for a cellar?*

Nine

WHILE ROSE AND PETER WERE BUSY AT PLAY, JIMMY delivered a pile of gently used clothes to the orphanage. They sat folded in the cellar when Peter returned. He was glad to change into a fresh shirt.

First he took his time in the bath, scrubbing himself with gently-used soap until his skin was pink. Even after the grime was gone, he did not feel clean or at peace; water and a sponge would not erase the dark memories tainting his dreams.

A mirror had been propped up against the tub. Peter stared at his reflection, combing his damp hair with his fingers, mulling over Rose's story. Her words had been powerful, and made him angry.

Of course she had struggled as a child in this sad place. He pictured her alone on that precipice, longing for a home that had been wrenched from her. Of course she would believe that nobody had searched for her.

It was a lie, though; Peter's father *did* search for Rose and her mother. He paid the best detectives available to find his late friend's wife and daughter. When years passed without any leads, Father surrendered to the possibility that both ladies were dead.

How could it be that none of the detectives were able to find a trace? They had been quick to take their money, but what of the work that had been entrusted to them?

That was a matter that Peter would settle later, when he returned home.

He wondered how long Mrs. Whittle would welcome him in her orphanage. He did not want to impose, but knew he couldn't return yet. Meredith would not yet be finished slandering him for his cowardice.

As he wondered how far the horse had taken him from civilization, there came a knock at the door.

"Are you finished?" It was Rose. "Dinner is ready."

"Yes." Peter cleared his throat, turning away from the mirror. How long had he been staring at himself?

Rose stepped inside, closing the door without making a sound. "I spoke to Mrs. Whittle, and indeed there will be no more hiding. You are welcome to join us in the dining room, if you wish."

"Of course," he said, a smile tugging at his lips. "I would be glad to meet them all."

Peter found himself distracted by her appearance. He hadn't thought she could look more beautiful. She had changed out of her black dress into one of deep purple which did her figure justice. Was he imagining that there was more color in her cheeks? It must be due to the sun, the hours they had spent playing together at the beach, as if time never separated them...

He must have been staring, for she blushed and said, "My black dress was covered in sand."

"Of course." He looked away, aware that he had gone a deep shade of red. "I didn't mean to be rude."

"No! Oh no, you aren't."

"I was raised not to stare."

"You can justify it by recalling that you hit your head," jested Rose.

Peter dared to look again. Earlier, her hair had been pulled into a strict knot; it was now braided back, airy and gentle.

Glancing at his clothes, he asked, "Do I look like a street urchin now?"

"No," Rose said. "You look…" She stopped herself before finishing flatly, "Tired from playing outside."

Peter wondered what it was that she had meant to say.

Between them settled a silence loaded with years of struggle and change. Despite this, he could feel a bond between them that hadn't died. They might have become different people, but they shared a childhood. Memories of games and laughter filled the gaps in their history.

Rose descended, lifting her skirts in the way society girls were taught. She had not forgotten these things, regardless of years in hiding. She had never stopped being Lady Rose.

"I wanted to ask my question," she said. "After all, I did win."

Peter would never admit that he had allowed her to win. He did so in hopes that she would stop treating him like a stranger; judging by how close she stood, the maneuver worked.

"What's your question, then?" he asked.

Rose turned away, holding her breath in a moment of hesitation.

At last she asked, "Why did you run away from home?

This cellar is a questionable place to hide from the world. Only something intolerable would drive you from the comforts of your home. I understand that things ended unpleasantly with that woman, but was it so terrible?"

Peter did not want to dwell on Meredith, but they had struck a deal at the beach. It was his fault, at any rate, for allowing her to win.

"You'll think me a coward if I tell you," he mumbled.

"My thoughts on cowardice have changed over the years."

Rose clasped her hands, and Peter once more resisted the urge to kiss them. She held herself with the dignity of Lord Finch's daughter. Embarrassing as the truth might be, he would answer her question because of who she was. Far be it from him to tell her a lie.

However, when he answered, he found it easier to look at the floor than her face. "I fled from the ball where I was to announce my engagement."

Peter braced himself for laughter, incredulity, some form of mockery. When no immediate reaction followed, he continued.

"I fled because my intended shoved me down a flight of stairs."

Rose faltered. "What?" she whispered. "Why?"

"I told her that I didn't want to marry her," he said. "I could not bear to think of a future by her side. I might have done it in a more...*courageous* manner..."

"Courage be *damned!*" she cried, startling him with the powerful word. "You are not bound to marry a cruel person!"

He continued in a near-whisper: "It didn't matter how often I saw her, I never truly knew her. She always appeared to be hiding something, concealing herself behind a smile. This act fooled most people, including my mother and sister. I shudder to imagine the things she's saying about me. She will use dark colors to paint her version of things."

Rose sat on a crate, staring angrily into a corner. "Do I know this lady?"

"I cannot say. Perhaps you met at some point." With a sigh, Peter finished his story. "I mounted a horse and left, never expecting to come here. It was a matter of fate. I do not think I would have visited this place voluntarily."

"Ironically, now you wish to stay," Rose said. "You're welcome to recover here; Mrs. Whittle said so. When you decide to return to your home—"

"That place is not home."

Peter sat on the crate across from her; the effort of remembering had exhausted him. He listened to the sounds of footsteps upstairs, as well as young girls' voices.

Again, he thought with indignation of Rose's story earlier. She was alive long after the world gave up on her, in a crowded place, hidden away.

"Is something expected of me upstairs?" he asked. "Has a story been prepared?"

Rose shook her head. "It is your choice," she said. "If you wish to omit your title, I will not correct you."

"Perhaps I will," he said. "I don't want to frighten people with a word. *Lord Everly.*" This last bit he mumbled, turning away.

"What happened to your father?" Rose asked.

Peter smirked. "Will I not have a turn to ask you something?" he inquired. "Or is tomorrow my day for questions?"

"You can ask anything," she said firmly, "after this."

"Father died one year ago, when his favorite ship

wrecked. The *August* had a special place in his heart; it was a wedding gift from my grandfather." Peter shook his head. "It was not a significant monetary loss to us, but Father could not bear the grief. His heart gave out."

"Money means nothing. You lost your father, and now…"

"I inherited the title," he said. "I don't know what to do with it."

"You also lost your home."

Before Rose could pursue the subject, he changed it. "Lady Rose, in honor of his memory, I must clarify that my father *did* search for you. He hired the best detectives the country had to offer. You and your mother were not forgotten."

"The detectives must not have wanted to come to this district," she said with a touch of anger, "regardless of their pay."

"Don't you think it odd?" Peter asked. "That I should be left at your door by an exhausted horse? Perhaps my father guided her. It's my turn to ask a question. When I return, will you come with me?"

The color once more drained from her face, and she cried, *"What?"*

"You belong in the place where you were born."

"You can't be serious."

"We've already proven that my mind is fine," he said. "I haven't lost my memory. I know what I want."

"What will people think? It's absurd!"

"You live in fear! This is no place for a lady."

"Yes," Rose whispered, "you're right. I am afraid. Perhaps I would accept your offer if the girls were not also afraid. I can't leave them behind because I was born into a golden cradle!"

"Will you think about it?" Peter implored—struck by the idea, he found himself unable to release it. "I will help you rebuild your life."

Rose stood before he had the opportunity to help her. "I will think about thinking about it," she said. He heard the punctuation mark; with this, she had ended the subject. "Let's go upstairs, if you're ready."

Ignoring the disappointment he felt, Peter filed his question away to ask again at a later time. He could not spend his life in this place, and did not intend to leave Rose alone.

With reluctance, he followed Rose upstairs to meet the pupils of Mrs. Whittle's Orphanage. He would rather have stayed in the cellar, staring at her.

Ten

Rose straightened her face as they ascended the stairs. Peter's offer had jarred her.

She knew that she had been unkind in the way that she rejected his offer. His entreaty was so bold that she was not able to remain calm. It was out of the question: Rose could not leave her pupils. Surely Peter would understand, being a rational man.

Rose would offer an apology later, nonetheless.

Emerging from the cellar, they heard Mrs. Whittle in the dining room, barking orders at the girls.

"Wait here," said Rose to Peter, who was trying to pat his hair into place. "I will tell her you're ready to step in."

He nodded without turning in her direction. Rose resisted the impulse to apologize on the spot. It was a conversation that must take place later, away from prying ears.

The table had been set, plates and silverware in order. With Peter's donation of cuff links, groceries had been purchased and Cook called back. She lurked in the kitchen, stirring the pot of stew one final time before serving.

There was an eager silence when Rose stepped into the dining room. The orphans looked at her with expectant eyes. They seldom had visitors for dinner; she found their eagerness endearing. Noting that they wore their best frocks, she swallowed her unease. Had Mrs. Whittle told them the status of their guest?

Rose had assured Peter that he could omit his title, but the girls were not dressed to greet an ordinary visitor. Their eyes sparkled more than usual. Peter might have to face his identity, after all. There was no time to inquire about it, with him standing in the hall.

"He's waiting," Rose told Mrs. Whittle, who turned to address the girls.

"In a line, shortest to tallest," she said in her clipped voice. "Marie, come here. You shall curtsy first and the others will follow."

Once all of the girls were in their designated spots, Mrs. Whittle turned to Rose with a nod. *Bring him in.*

Rose returned to Peter, who stood lost in a train of thought. She touched his arm, startling him out of the reverie.

"I think the girls know what you are. They're preparing to curtsy," she whispered. "I didn't want it to startle you."

If Peter was disappointed, he masked it well. "Thank you," he said. "Lead the way, please."

Rose glanced at his face in the flickering light and saw determination. It made her curious and uneasy. Instinct told her he had only accepted her *no* for the moment. He would later ask again the question about leaving, and he would be more persuasive.

It was a matter she would handle in due time.

Peter stepped into the dining room, blinking in the candlelight. Turning, he smiled at the line of eager young girls, opening his mouth to speak. Before he could say a word, Marie bobbed into a flawless curtsy; like an ocean wave, the other girls mimicked her. They did so perfectly; only eight-year-old Anne wobbled when dipping her knees.

"I wanted to show you," said Mrs. Whittle, "that you are not in the presence of savages. You'll recognize the order in which we've set the table. The forks and spoons are where they ought to be. As the guest, you will take the seat at the end."

"I am charmed to meet you all," said Peter with a bow. "Thank you for such great hospitality."

Marie ushered the girls to their seats. Some of them wore crooked smiles; others appeared too nervous to meet Peter's gaze.

Marie looked at Rose and flashed her a mischievous smile; doubtless, she approved of Peter's appearance. Rose glared, hoping that she would not be teased by her friend at the dinner table.

As Rose's roommate, Marie was the only soul aside from Mrs. Whittle who knew of her past. Marie had been in their shared bedroom when Rose entered, wearing a dress covered in sand.

"You're late," Marie had said. "Rose—are you *smiling?* Who is it?"

How telling that her question had not been *what happened?* but *who is it?*

After learning that Mrs. Whittle's guest was a figure from Rose's past, Marie insisted that she look elegant for dinner. Perhaps she had overdone it; Rose was dressed for a dinner party, while Peter had arrived in Jimmy's hand-me-downs. To Peter's credit, he did not seem to care.

Rose indicated the chair reserved for Peter, but he did not sit. "Which is your chair?" he asked.

Rose shrugged her shoulders. Seating arrangements often changed; Mrs. Whittle knew where Rose was to be at the table that night.

As though reading her mind, Peter turned to Mrs. Whittle. "Where is Lady Rose sitting?" he asked.

Rose flinched at his words—*Lady Rose.*

One of the girls, startled, dropped her napkin and silverware. It caused a resounding crash which made the others jump.

Lady Rose.

Marie's jaw dropped, her manners forgotten in the tension of the moment. Of all the pupils, only she had known Rose's secret. Now the title had been announced, albeit accidentally, to everyone.

Rose could not be angry with Peter. He hadn't known it to be a secret in the house. Mrs. Whittle seemed to have prompted the slip with her exaggerated dinner preparations.

Unapologetic, Mrs. Whittle indicated the seat to Peter's right. He drew the chair and looked at Rose, waiting for her to sit.

Rose clasped her hands, unable to reel in her emotions. Even if he had known her title to be a secret, Peter was determined that she should be treated as *Lady Rose.*

There was no being rid of stubborn Peter, and Rose could not be sure that she wished him to go.

"Thank you, sir," she said, managing to ignore the girls' piercing stares.

Mrs. Whittle's wan smile did not fade as, true to his character, Peter helped Rose settle onto her chair.

She watched him, battling her frustration. She had suggested openness by telling him that Mother was friends with Mrs. Whittle. Never had she implied that, in the orphanage, Lady Rose did not exist.

Because of Peter, that had changed.

Stubborn Peter, she thought, taking a deep breath. *Optimistic Peter.*

Maddening Peter.

"I hope you feel better, Lord Everly," said Mrs. Whittle, taking from Rose the burden of conversation. "We have prepared a bedroom upstairs. I won't have you sleeping on a cot."

Peter smiled. "You needn't have gone to such great lengths for me."

"Hospitality is an art," said Mrs. Whittle, as Cook came in with the pot of stew. "If you stay longer than those cufflinks are worth, we'll put you to work. Do you know how to fix a door hinge?"

"Mrs. Whittle," Rose found herself saying, "Jimmy does that. You wouldn't take away his chores. They give the old man purpose."

"*Lady Rose,*" said Mrs. Whittle, watching Cook ladle stew into each bowl, "Jimmy has enough to do at home. Perhaps you are good with a gun?" she asked Peter. "The night watch could use help."

"I go shooting sometimes," he said.

"We will not put him in danger!" Rose cried. She would not have Peter—stubborn, optimistic, maddening Peter—left outside to face arsonists.

Cook broke the silence, ladling a second helping of stew into Peter's bowl. He did not notice, eyes fixed on Rose.

"Very well," said Mrs. Whittle. "He and I can talk later. *Lady Rose,* it is remarkable how you resemble your mother tonight."

"Thank you," Rose said, somewhat mollified. Her mother had been a beautiful woman. If Marie's choice of clothing made Rose look like Lady Finch, it was something to be glad for.

"Let us eat," said Mrs. Whittle, and it seemed that she was finished playing cat-and-mouse with Rose and Peter. "It would be a shame if this meal went cold. Thank you, My Lord, for providing it."

"It's an honor," he said. "I am glad to meet your pupils."

Rose looked at the girls. They sat in their best dresses, which in truth were well-loved frocks without stains. Layers of graying lace gave them shabby elegance. The orphans had nothing new with which to greet Lord Everly, but they tried nonetheless.

Did Peter realize how fascinating he was to those children?

Sensing Peter's stare, Rose turned. In his expression lurked the question he asked in the cellar. *Come back with me?*

She saw stubbornness in the set of his jaw.

I will wait here, the look told her, *until you decide.*

Eleven

Meredith regretted having asked Grumbacher that question, for the answer had been *at once.* Lord Bannister wouldn't keep her for another day. So eager was he to be rid of her that he commanded the servants to pack her trunk after she left her room that morning.

After the mockery of a proposal, Meredith had sat numbly through tea, listening to Grumbacher boast about investments. Meanwhile, her wardrobe and drawers upstairs were being emptied, her things cleared away.

Having finished tea, she had stepped outside to find her trunks being secured onto Grumbacher's carriage. She should not have been surprised, yet the sight shocked her into silence.

Lord Bannister had emptied his home of all evidence that she existed, treating her as if she were dead.

Meredith swallowed a lump in her throat. She would not sacrifice her dignity by begging him to keep her for one more day. What was more, she had a niggling fear that, should she disobey his orders, she would be stabbed in her sleep. Such was his desperation to be rid of her.

He would stab me. I would be truly dead.

A suspicion unfolded in her mind that she couldn't ignore, one regarding her mother and the circumstances surrounding her death.

Storing her suspicion for later reflection, Meredith dared to voice a request.

"I wondered if Ava might accompany me," she told Lord Bannister, trying for a voice of meekness. "She is my maid, and she knows all about me."

It would be too frightening, too troublesome, for Meredith to befriend another ladies' maid the way she'd done with Ava. Theirs was a bond formed over the course of years...

"Ridiculous," said Lord Bannister, and her suspicion reared up once more in her mind.

He would kill me, Meredith thought, *to be rid of me...* She looked at the portrait of Mother. Lord Bannister ordered that it be hung on the dining room wall, over the spot where Meredith found her lifeless body.

To be rid of me...

"Miss Smith was hired to work in my house," said Lord Bannister. "I'm sending *you* with Silas. That is enough of a burden."

Grumbacher joined them. "What's this?" he asked, straightening his tie. Meredith hated the triumph on his insect-like face. "A request for me? Let's hear it, then." A command—no *please.*

"It's nothing," said Lord Bannister, but Meredith cut him off.

"I want Ava." This time she directed her words at Grumbacher. "My ladies' maid. Lord Bannister seems to think you would take issue with it."

Grumbacher loosened his tie, forcing Meredith to wait while he considered her words.

"The mansion is large," he said, "and I don't see that an extra hired hand can do much harm. If the maid wishes to come, she is welcome."

"She will," Meredith said eagerly. "I need only talk to her."

Lord Bannister quickly erased her smile by saying, "Miss Smith is *my* hired help. I will talk to her. I'll only be gone for a moment."

Her heart sank as he hurried upstairs. Ava would not come if Lord Bannister made the request, for he would not make it a request.

He would make it a threat.

It should not have hurt, then, to find herself alone in a carriage with Grumbacher. Clutching at her reticule, she stared at his mansion as it came into view. It was wide rather than tall, built of gloomy brown stone, and filled with secrets she would have to learn to live with.

No words had been said during the trip, but she was not oblivious to how Grumbacher stared at her. He puffed at a pungent-smelling pipe, holding it out of the window to clear the carriage of its smoke.

As they neared the building, Grumbacher spoke. "The West Wing has been prepared for your comfort."

Meredith fixed her gaze out of the window, not gracing him with a look.

"It provides the best view of the plains. Do not worry about your maid—you will be provided with another. The servants have been informed that you will be treated as the lady of this house."

"How can that be," she heard herself ask, "if I am not yet married into it?"

"About that," said Grumbacher, after a stretch. "There are certain—ah—things that must be taken care of."

"Which things?" Meredith asked, but the carriage stopped, ending their conversation.

A servant opened the carriage door, bowing his head to greet the master of the house. Meredith waited for Grumbacher to exit, but he did not, crossing one leg over the other.

"The servants will show you to the West Wing," he said, making a vague gesture with his pipe. "I will return next week. Feel free to tell me if anything displeases you."

"You aren't coming in?" Meredith asked.

Grumbacher pondered before leaning back, holding his pipe out of the window.

"Let us have one matter clarified," he said, using the tone she often heard from Lord Bannister, the one that implied she was a simple-minded girl who needed things explained to her. "I do not sleep here. I sleep elsewhere. You needn't ask for details, as I will not give them."

Meredith could not decide if this ought to be taken as a blessing or an insult. He slept elsewhere—yet she had been stripped of a life, believing that at some point she would be Mrs. Grumbacher. Before the unfairness could sink in, she slid out of the carriage, marching past servants carrying her trunks, trying to reach the door.

"Oh," called Grumbacher, and she stopped. "Careful not

to enter the East Wing, Daughter of the Sea. If your curiosity should lead to places not meant for you—well, you will regret stepping out of line. Good night."

Daughter of the Sea. Mermaid. It had been her title since birth, her curse since conception. She would never be Mrs. Grumbacher, never Mrs. anything.

She listened as the carriage door closed, heard it pull down the same path that had brought her. It swept Grumbacher to some woman's home, perhaps her bed, a place where he would have company. Meanwhile, Meredith stood alone in front of a big house.

She did not realize someone was speaking until they touched her shoulder. "Miss? *Miss?*"

Meredith looked up. Her eyes focused on one of the servants. In the dark she could not gauge his age, only that he was fairly tall and had a ragged appearance.

She glared—he looked at her and saw *Mermaid,* so why bother feigning kindness? "What is it?"

If he heard her anger, he did not acknowledge it. "You have been standing outside for a long time," he said, "and the servants are waiting to show you to your rooms."

She shook her shoulder free from his hand.

"Are these steps among the places I am not allowed to visit?" she demanded. "Like the East Wing? Don't touch me again, I am warning you!"

The man looked at her with something akin to regret. Knowing she was behaving exactly as the staff expected of her, Meredith pushed past him and into the mansion.

In this mansion, she had been promised to Grumbacher as a girl. She had cried and screamed when forced to lift her skirts for him to see the scales over her knee. When they released her, she fled outside, collapsing onto the grass.

Years later, she found herself abandoned in the very place that she loathed.

Lady Meredith's act was useless in Grumbacher's mansion; she could not pretend to be anything but what she was. His servants knew of her curse. In this place, she was defenseless.

She crashed into a woman in a gray frock whose sunken eyes were corpse-like.

"Welcome to Grumbacher house," said the woman as Meredith took a step back. "My name is Mrs. Gourd and I am the housekeeper. Would you care for a tour of the place?"

"No," Meredith said, packing her anger and fear into one word. "I want to go to my room. Show me to my wing, where I am *allowed* to be, and you need not worry about me."

Mrs. Gourd narrowed those eyes before nodding. She motioned for Meredith to follow her up the stairs. They passed portraits of people so lifelike, it felt as if they could read Meredith's thoughts. She shivered.

She was led through a set of double-doors into a sitting room. A fire flickered in the hearth; across from it were two soft armchairs.

"Your room is at the end of the hall," she heard the housekeeper say. "Your things have been unpacked. There is a tray with food on the table. Ring the bell if you need anything—"

"Leave," Meredith whispered. "The only thing I need is for you to leave."

A pause ensued. At last she heard the housekeeper's keys rattle as the woman made her exit, heard the *click* when the door closed. Meredith waited for the sound of a lock, but it did not come. She was free, then, but a prisoner.

She sank to her knees, staring into the fire. Her life had reached its inevitable end, leaving her in the home of her nightmares.

If I had begged Peter, she found herself thinking. *I could have told him why I needed him. He would have had mercy if he'd known—he is a better person than me—I only needed to be honest.*

Her storm of thoughts continued, pointless. At last she was forced to accept that Peter would not have cared, even if he'd known of the fate that awaited her. Why should he?

Twelve

"YOU ARE A FOOL," MEREDITH HAD SAID.

Peter did not dream of the fall. Instead he saw the look on her face in the instant before she shoved him. The memory returned with extraordinary clarity.

Her expression had been one of anger, but also fear—the fear of a trapped animal. He had been so occupied with Rose that there hadn't been time to dwell on Meredith's strange behavior.

Peter steeled himself. Meredith's expression was of no concern to him; he did not want her in his mind.

A knock sounded at the door, stirring him from the reverie.

Peter blinked in the sunlight, noticing that the window was open. Through the billowing curtains drifted a fresh ocean breeze.

He had not opened the window, having slept the night through. Did somebody enter while he rested?

He sat up, wiping sweat from his face, and hurried to the door.

Mrs. Whittle waited on the other side, holding a tray of breakfast. "Good afternoon, My Lord," she said, walking into the bedroom.

"Afternoon?" he repeated.

"Yes, you've had your share of sleep today. Close the door, I want to talk to you."

Peter wondered if he ought to be worried, but Mrs. Whittle said this with the cheery voice of a nanny, so he complied.

She placed the tray on an old wooden dresser which swayed precariously under its weight. He watched coffee spill from the cup; Mrs Whittle did not seem to notice. She motioned for him to sit at the edge of the bed, taking the wooden chair for herself.

"First things first. Are you feeling better? Do you have a headache?"

"No headache, thank you."

"I am impressed," said Mrs. Whittle. "You're stronger than most men I've met. You fell off a horse and hours later went to play at the beach."

"Thank you," Peter said.

Her smile was calming. The orphanage might not have been his home, but she spoke as though he belonged in her family.

"What is it you wanted to talk about?" he asked.

"It's about Rose. *Lady* Rose, if you will." Mrs. Whittle corrected herself with a smirk.

Peter's face fell at the mention of Rose. After dinner, she had vanished into the kitchen, not speaking a single word to him. When she didn't return, he retired to bed, uncomfortable with the younger girls' scrutiny.

Peter suspected that he had made Rose angry, but didn't

know how. Mrs. Whittle might be able to enlighten him.

She continued before he could ask. "We must finish our chat from last night. I understand you want to make yourself useful." Mrs. Whittle smiled. "Alas, Lady Rose seems rather protective of you."

Peter hoped her keen eyes would not perceive how his heart raced at the thought.

"I do think you capable of using a hammer," said Mrs. Whittle. "I won't put you to work, but you'll grow bored with nothing to do."

"Bored? I doubt it," he admitted. "This place is so different. I never thought I'd find myself here."

"Perhaps the most useful thing you can do for us is observe. I don't think anyone else of your social stature will be dropped here by a tired horse."

"I don't want to take up space."

"Help yourself to this space," she said. "Take note of what you see. Only then will you wish to help."

Peter wondered what Mrs. Whittle was asking. Did she hope he would take the place of Rose's father? Lord Julian had been killed for wanting to help. Though flattered to be compared with a man he'd admired, Peter did not think himself capable. He had not even been able to tell a woman to leave him be.

"I don't think you *could* return home and forget us," Mrs. Whittle said. "You're stronger than that."

"Few would take me seriously. I did not vanish from society in a graceful manner."

"You misunderstand," Mrs. Whittle said. "I'm not asking you to mimic Lord Finch. Nobody wants you dead! Heavens, you're far too young. I beg you not to do anything rash."

"What would you like me to do, then?"

Mrs. Whittle glanced at the window, hesitating. When at last she spoke, there was pain in her words. "You want to take Rose from this place."

Peter did not know whether to apologize for this truth. He listened, holding his tongue. She had chosen this conversation topic for a reason.

"My eldest," Mrs. Whittle continued, "the one that I swore to protect. You want to take her."

Though her words held no accusation, he found himself reacting defensively. "Even if so, I don't think it will happen. She won't talk about returning with me, so you needn't worry."

"Keep trying."

Peter stared, dumbstruck.

"On her sickbed, Arabella told me to protect her daughter. I hired Lady Rose to teach so that she would not feel out of place, but this isn't her home. I believe she's averse to your offer because of a fear in her heart."

Mrs. Whittle's shoulders slumped.

"Rose is loyal. That's not the reason why she thinks she must stay. Whenever I speak to her about the future, I realize she's given up. She's settled for teaching at an orphanage, but she is capable of much more. I cannot let her choose a life of drudgery if she has a better option. I love her too much."

"You *want* me to take her," he said slowly.

"She is not like the other pupils," explained Mrs. Whittle. "She was not born in this place and has never been accustomed to such a life. I cannot bear to see her scavenge for stale bread, day after day." He saw moisture in her eyes as she finished. "She belongs where she was born. My rose won't bloom in a foul place. If you don't convince her to leave, no one will."

Peter felt the weight of her request. It was difficult to imagine himself convincing Rose of anything if she continued to hide in the kitchen.

"She's angry with me," he said. "She vanished last night. I wasn't able to tell her good-night."

"Is she angry?" asked Mrs. Whittle, her smile returning. "You showed up from out of the blue. She is trying to conceal her strong feelings for you."

"How do you know?"

"I saw her face, as well. What you interpreted as anger I know to be quite different." Mrs. Whittle stood and took the tray from the dresser, offering it to him. "I will not deny that she is stubborn."

He accepted the tray. "I fear that if I ask her the question again I'll be slapped."

"Then don't use words," said Mrs. Whittle. "You have much to learn about women. You'll find her in the garden, where she is attempting to hide from you."

"How do you think I could make a difference, then?" he asked, frustrated.

"She is also hoping you will find your way outside." Mrs. Whittle turned away. "You cannot talk her into leaving. She's too intelligent; her mind will not be changed by words. Find a way to change her heart."

She opened the door and stepped out, leaving him to his thoughts.

He sipped his coffee, wondering once more how the window had come to be opened. Someone must have entered while he slept—that was the only explanation.

If Mrs. Whittle was telling the truth, Peter *did* have a

great deal to learn. Accustomed to forceful Meredith, he did not know how to speak with Rose. She was different, making herself small so that others could grow.

How could Peter win the confidence of this rose? He had already been pricked by her thorns.

Mrs. Whittle advised that he change her heart, not her mind. Perhaps that had been his mistake.

Roses should be handled with care.

Thirteen

"Is he still sleeping?" Marie asked, hanging a dress on the clothesline. "Or did we frighten him last night? He vanished after dinner."

Rose focused on the meager garden patch. She tore a stubborn weed from dry soil, wishing that Marie would change the subject. She had gone outside to organize her thoughts, but Marie was determined to keep Peter in them.

"Perhaps he isn't feeling well," she said, tossing the weed into a bag of rubbish.

Rose's attempt to explain his absence did not ease her guilt. She should not have gone to the kitchen after dinner. Mrs. Whittle's teasing and the pupils' stares had become overwhelming; her retreat had been a desperate bid for privacy. She must have stayed much longer than intended, for Peter was gone when she finished.

Rose did not mean to hurt him, but his appearance upended all she was accustomed to. She did not know who to be, could not decide between past and present.

"It seemed he was slipping away," said Marie, reaching

for a clothespin. "Cook didn't *need* help with the dishes, you know."

Rose turned to glare at Marie. "Don't judge me! You don't know what this is like! Yesterday I was no one, giving embroidery lessons to little girls. This morning, I woke up as *Lady Rose.*"

"You didn't need to stop being Lady Rose," said Marie, unflinching.

"My mother told me our titles were gone. We came to disappear. You know what happened to my father!"

"What I mean is that you never stopped being Lady Rose to Peter. You could be fair to him and not resort to hiding."

"I am not hiding," Rose lied. "I haven't cleaned out the garden in weeks."

"None of this is a surprise to me," Marie said.

It was true. Rose had confided her past to Marie; it was easier than coming up with a story. The years they spent as roommates created a great bond between them.

"I know what you were before," Marie continued. "I also know the person you are now. If he isn't feeling well, shouldn't you check on him? I thought he was your patient."

"I checked this morning," she said, reaching for a shovel. "He was sleeping."

Rose had gone to see her patient before sunrise, only to find him deep in slumber. The May heat made the bedroom stuffy, so she opened the window. She had stared at Peter's face before leaving, puzzled by the storm in her heart. She knew her attitude to him was unkind, but did not know how else to behave.

"Isn't that convenient?" Marie asked. "What do you do when avoiding someone? Visit when they're sleeping and can't ask questions. I cannot for the life of me understand your behavior. He's a gentleman, he's kind, he's handsome..."

"Marie," Rose cut her off, "he..." *He wants me to go with him.* She trailed off, unable to form the words.

"He's here," Marie said cheerfully, causing Rose to stiffen. "Good afternoon, My Lord."

Rose took a deep breath. She turned to see Marie curtsying to Peter. He had wandered into the garden, stopping in a patch of sunlight.

"Good afternoon," he said to Marie. "You needn't curtsy."

"I have to practice sometime, don't I?" Marie replied. With a bright smile she added, "Lady Rose needs help in the garden."

"I don't need help," Rose heard herself say. "I know how to dig."

She bit her tongue and turned away. Why couldn't she be kind? None of it was his fault.

Peter had not missed the edge to her words. Tucking his hands into his pockets, he asked, "What shall I do then? Gather flowers?"

Marie smirked, returning to her work.

Rose got to her feet, taking off the gardening gloves. "You could gather flowers," she said, "or you can rest, like you're supposed to be doing."

"I've had enough rest," he said. "Give me something to fix and a hammer."

She smiled. "Nothing needs fixing today."

"I beg to differ," Peter said. "I have seen quite a lot of things here that need fixing."

"They cannot be fixed with a hammer."

He said nothing, watching her with an intense gaze. The

silence that ensued spoke volumes—and was so loud that Marie heard it.

"The kitchen garden can wait," she said. "You two go walking. I won't tell."

Rose wiped her hands on her apron. The thought of being alone with him made her afraid—not for her sake, but his. She could not control the words that came out of her mouth. Frustration overpowered her.

Peter smiled. "Where are the wildflowers?" he asked.

"Did I make you angry last night?" Peter asked as they strolled through a clearing.

"No," she said under her breath. "You didn't."

"Then why did you vanish?"

Rose stopped. It was the perfect moment to admit how pathetic she had become. "I don't know who I am, Peter. It isn't anything you did."

"I know who you are."

Peter spoke with certainty that Rose wished she could share. He never had a reason to change his identity or doubt it. Perhaps he assumed things were similar for her, but Rose only felt certain of *his* identity. He was stubborn, loyal, and…

Maddening.

"I hope you feel better," she said. "You needed rest."

"I'm not in pain."

The answer was vague enough that she knew something troubled him. When he continued, Rose understood why.

"Mrs. Whittle said I can stay for as long as I like. I wanted to make sure it wouldn't bother you."

Rose could not deny the relief and—yes, happiness—the news brought her. If he stayed for long enough, perhaps she *would* believe his words; if he stayed, she might come to terms with herself.

"I hope I haven't given you the wrong impression, Peter. Your presence doesn't bother me." *It confuses me to no end.*

"I suppose you did. What with the hiding and all."

"I wasn't hiding from you." She wrung her apron nervously. "You have to understand. I—I stopped feeling like *Lady Rose* years ago."

"That doesn't mean you stopped being her." Peter offered a crooked smile. "If you prefer it, I will try not to use the title."

"I think—that might help. Thank you."

"Very good, *Miss* Rose," Peter said.

She felt a rush of excitement, hearing him pronounce her Christian name. What was more, he said it as if it were a beautiful sound, a prayer.

"How long do you think it will take for me to recover?" he asked. "I won't be leaving alone, you know." Before she could answer, he strolled into the flowers.

Maddening, she thought, hurrying after him.

"I don't know what I was expecting," he said. "Flowers here are no different than they are at home." Picking one, he peered at it. "A common daisy. Why are we taught that these places are different?"

"To discourage you from visiting," she said. "You admitted that you wouldn't have come if the horse hadn't thrown you off."

"That's true enough."

Peter looked at her, offering the daisy. Her heart raced.

Was the daisy a gift, or was he asking her to identify it, like they had done as children?

"You called it a daisy," she said, settling on the latter. "I think it looks like one, too."

He smiled and said, "I can't give a rose a rose, can I?"

"Thank you," she managed, accepting the gift.

Daisies were common, but the one Peter gave her had become inexplicably prettier than all of the others she had seen.

"I should be thanking you," he said. "I interrupted your life. I wouldn't blame you for wishing me gone."

"No!" she said too quickly. "Don't feel pressured to leave." *I'd like for you to stay.* "I won't hide again. You *must* promise me one thing, though."

"What's that?"

"Don't let Mrs. Whittle talk you into joining the night watch! For goodness' sake, I don't recognize her. The people who live here are in danger when they join. I don't doubt that you can shoot, but this is different."

She wondered at the smile on his face.

"All right," he said. "I won't join the watch, but I need to do something. I'm not bound to the cellar anymore. What good does it do to sit around?"

"You can..." She stared at the daisy, thinking. "Well... there's a piano. I remember you had talent with music."

"Yes," he said, the smile not fading.

"It's out of tune, but I know you can work with it. Perhaps you could play melodies during the girls' singing lessons. It would be a welcome change from my mediocre playing."

"I doubt your playing is mediocre," he said.

"It won't be as good as yours. I was..." Rose choked on

the words. "The piano at my father's house...I did not have much time to practice on it before he was..."

He cut her off. "I understand, Rose. No need to stir up the past."

"A bit of music could liven up the house. If someone else is playing, I can focus on their voices."

"I'm happy to help," he said.

"Tonight, then?"

"Tonight. I wonder, could I have some paper? I want to send a letter."

"There is plenty of paper," Rose said, glad that he made a request she could accept. "I'll have Jimmy take your letter to the post."

"I'd like to do it," Peter said, as they turned back to the orphanage. "A chance to walk about."

"Yes, it would be nice." Rose sighed. "We don't have a post office, unfortunately."

"Why not?"

"No one wants to come in," she said. "Not even the post-man. Everyone must cross the border for important letters."

Her words were met with silence.

At last he said, voice sharp with anger, "There is much that needs to be fixed here. You're right, though. It can't be done with a hammer."

Rose sensed his restlessness for change and found it unnerving. What was the stubborn young man thinking?

She hoped he would not do anything rash. If so, was there anything she could say to stop him?

Fourteen

THE NEXT MORNING, MEREDITH HAD BEEN AWAKE FOR AN hour when there was a knock at the door. She groaned, lacking the spirit to see anyone.

"What is it?" she asked, hoping it was not the housekeeper.

The door opened. A housemaid stepped in, carrying a breakfast tray. If she noticed Meredith's ill temper, she did not acknowledge it. Instead, she dipped into a perfect, silent curtsy.

Meredith watched the young maid cross the room and open the window. She sat up, resisting an urge to close the curtains of the four-poster. How dare they barge in and expect her to start *living*—as if all was well, as if she had not been handed away like an unwanted chair?

The maid continued to work in silence, shaking curtains, sending clouds of dust in the air.

She must be ignoring me, thought Meredith, *like everyone else does.*

Turning, the maid pointed to her throat with a look of apology.

This at last piqued Meredith's interest. "You cannot talk?" she asked.

The maid shook her head. *No.*

Even as Meredith's anger faded, questions raced through her mind. Why couldn't the maid talk? Was she another one of Grumbacher's oddities, or did her muteness stem from something else? She also wondered if they had assigned her a mute maid on purpose.

The maid's apologetic smile did not fade as she approached the wardrobe. She fixed Meredith with an expectant look.

Meredith understood: She would have to state what she wished to wear. There would be no advice like that which Ava used to offer.

"Something dark, I think," she said, standing and facing the window. It might have been a sunny day, but her heart felt dark indeed.

Meredith looked down at the plains. In any other place she might have thought their verdure beautiful. Trapped in Grumbacher's cage, she saw only bars stretching on without end. The green offered no place to hide.

"There is a dark blue dress," she said over her shoulder. "I will wear that one."

As the maid searched through the wardrobe, Meredith looked into her trunks. A puzzle box had been packed in one of them, partly hidden by colorful scarves.

Meredith had forgotten about the box. It was a gift from Mother, one she hadn't touched in years. She took it and traced the carved surface, searching for the hidden knobs. Pressing them, she heard a *click* as the lid popped open.

She gasped. In the box were her mother's jewels—pearls and rings, bracelets and pendants. On top of these sat a note in Ava's neat hand: *These belong to you. Good luck, friend.*

Meredith's lip trembled. How she missed Ava! She knew that, if Bannister hadn't interfered, Ava would have accompanied her. It would have been selfish, though, to bring Ava into captivity.

Meredith chose her string of pearls and closed the box, placing it in the trunk once more.

Behind her stood the new maid, waiting. There was sadness in her smile. She knew well that her presence was disappointing.

Meredith felt a stirring of sympathy. *Perhaps I can have a friend here too.*

"I would like to wear these today," she said, holding out the pearls, "if you could help me."

It would not matter if nobody saw; Meredith chose to dress well. She would not wander the mansion looking like the deranged monster Grumbacher's servants expected.

AFTER DRESSING, Meredith stepped into the corridor.

Although the maid could not introduce herself, she had done her work well. She made art with Meredith's hair, braiding it into a style more elegant than Ava ever managed.

Meredith's gaze drifted to the East Wing. She stared at the dark half of the mansion; it appeared to be immersed in nighttime. Grumbacher's words surfaced in her mind: *You will regret having gone.*

Shaking her head, she descended the stairs. Exploring the East Wing was out of the question. Recalling the nature of Grumbacher's collection, she preferred not to glimpse that night-world.

She trailed her hand along the wall as she descended the stairs. *Lady of the house.* Was it a meaningful title when she had no one to entertain? Could she be *lady of the house* if she did not know the name of her own maid?

Meredith crossed the floor of black-and-white tiles. Opening the front door, she stepped onto the veranda in search of fresh air. The ocean of green rolled on for miles. She wondered if there was a stable; it might be enjoyable to go for a horseback ride.

Who could she ask? Her maid would not be able to provide a satisfactory answer.

While pondering the matter, she noticed someone stepping around the house. He carried a large, wrapped parcel. It was the man who had touched her shoulder the night before.

Seeing him in the light of day, she pegged him to be older than her, in his late twenties. He wore battered clothing and his hat was in tatters, but he held his head up regardless.

Meredith regretted having barked at him. She thought of going back inside, but he spotted her and smiled.

"Good morning," he said, carrying the parcel up the steps. "I'm here with the post. I won't bother you."

"No," she said, tired. "Don't worry. You were here before me."

The man propped the parcel against the door, wiping his hands on his trousers.

Meredith waited for him to speak, turning once more to the plains. If he had something to say, she would listen.

There was no point in continuing to resist; all of her battles were lost.

"Are you all right?" was his question.

How odd to hear those four words. No one in the past had cared.

"What does it mean to be all right?" Meredith replied. "You tell me and perhaps I will be able to answer."

He stepped nearer. "If you like the veranda, I can place a table outside for you. Fresh air makes me feel better."

She wondered that he should offer to do anything for her. "A table," she mumbled. "Yes, that might be nice. I don't intend to be inside all day."

"Will do, then," said the man kindly. "I know there's one in storage. I can bring it around."

Meredith turned. There was something familiar about his face. Logic argued that she could not, in her life, have known someone with a smile so transparent.

"Thank you," Meredith said. "I wonder if you can tell me the name of my maid—the one who cannot speak."

"Her name is Agnes. To be fair, I've never been certain that she *can't* speak. I suspect she won't. A deep hurt, perhaps, made her silent."

Meredith nodded. "And your name? I'm sorry I did not ask before."

"My name is Gideon," he said.

Gideon. It sounded familiar.

"What is your work here?" she asked. "Are you the postman? The groundskeeper?"

"I don't exactly work here," he admitted.

She frowned, but could not push the subject without sounding rude.

"You've seen me before, Lady Meredith," he said, startling her with the sound of her title. "I don't blame you for erasing that day from your mind. You were crying on the grass."

Meredith crossed her arms, trying to remember. *Gideon...Gideon.*

She remembered the day she had been brought here, as a six-year-old child. After being forced to reveal her leg, she had dashed out the front door to cry. There was a boy on the grass; he had been older, on the cusp of manhood.

That day, he introduced herself in the same way he'd done now: *My name is Gideon.*

"You were the youth sitting on the grass," she whispered.

"I was fourteen at the time. I'd been here for three years. We were both..." He struggled for words. "Lost."

"Are you a servant?" she persisted.

Gideon shook his head. "More than a servant, less than a relative." He specified, reluctantly: "Unacknowledged bastard child. The only reason he keeps me is because I know too much."

"Then we are kindred spirits," she said. "I'm sorry for being rude last night."

"Don't apologize. I can't blame you for your reaction to being left here. I've thought of leaving, but don't have anywhere to go." Gideon took a step back. "Wait here. I will bring your table."

Meredith watched him leave, confused. The last thing she'd expected to find in this mansion was kindness—but how long would it last?

Could she trust Gideon, truly?

~

THE TABLE GIDEON brought to the veranda spoke of aged elegance. It was small; Meredith guessed it would only seat two people. The surface was of sturdy wood. She imagined that, once polished, it would be a fine bit of décor.

Such things had once interested her, when she visited acquaintances and judged their furnishing choices. It was not important anymore; it was simply something for her to ponder as she sat alone, watching the sky darken.

Smoothing the surface with her hand, she wondered how much time had passed since Gideon brought the table and its accompanying chair. He slipped away after that, saying that he needed to trim some hedges.

Meredith had watched him vanish around the large house, wishing she had thought to bring a book.

She heard the door open behind her and did not need to turn; instinct told her that it was the housekeeper.

"Would you like your tea brought outside, Lady Meredith?" asked Mrs. Gourd.

Meredith did not turn; she would rather not look into those lifeless eyes. Why was it that everything Grumbacher came into contact with had distasteful qualities?

"I suppose," she said. "And I assume you know that I need salt in my water."

In the silence that ensued, she sensed the housekeeper's indignation at being spoken to in such a manner. She could not blame the woman; with a face frightening as that, it was unlikely that the maids would often talk back.

"Yes," said Mrs. Gourd, "Mr. Grumbacher instructed me of your...requirement."

Meredith scoffed. *Requirement.* What a tasteful manner in which to refer to the things a Mermaid needed. She did not expect to find much respect under this roof for being Mer; in return, she would not offer courtesy where it was lacked.

"Tea will be brought out shortly," Mrs. Gourd said, words clipped, and soon came the sound of the front door closing.

Meredith found herself smiling. *Small victories.* How tired she was of allowing others to step on her. She'd had enough of that for the rest of her life.

The sighing of the wind reminded her of a hollow that she felt in her chest. It was not a new emptiness; it began caving in shortly after she found her mother's body. As the years crept by, the emptiness continued to deepen. She managed to conceal it with her grandiose acts, finding distraction in the attention of gentleman at social events. It was not true distraction, though, not fulfilling, for her heart longed to go with one of them, and she had never been allowed to fall.

A hot tear slid down her face. She wiped at it impatiently; too late to be weak now. At last she had been abandoned in the place for which she'd been destined all of her life. There was nothing more to be done about it.

Meredith composed herself and waited for tea.

It was during that wait that Gideon reappeared. He held his tattered hat in his hand, lifting it in greeting as he darted across the plain to the house. Meredith tried not to smile; his hair was in disorder, and something of his appearance brought her mirth.

"You're still outside," he said, ascending the steps, taking two at a time. "You weren't joking. Well, I wouldn't want to spend a day in there, either."

He smelled earthy, like the hedge he had gone off to

trim. Meredith wondered where he had come from. How did he survive, alone in Grumbacher house for most of his life? In his green eyes, there was a spark of optimism. She could believe that he was *happy* about having trimmed a hedge. Such good spirits surely did not belong in the area.

"The housekeeper has gone to fetch my tea," Meredith told him, for lack of anything more substantial to say. "Maybe—maybe you would like some."

Because he had been working; surely he was hungry.

Because it was warm out; surely he was dehydrated.

Because she was desperate for company, and if sharing her tea with Gideon would keep him around, she would give him all of it.

Gideon leaned on the table, running a hand through that messy hair. "I smell like a tree," he reminded her.

Meredith said nothing. Her invitation was a desperate bid to try and calm the storm inside of her. It was a hope that his presence would fill in the silence otherwise only broken by wind.

"Of course," he added, perhaps seeing her despair. "If you'll have me, I'll be glad to join you—but I'll have to vanish until tea comes out."

"Why?" she asked, as he turned to hoist himself over the banister—effortlessly, as though he had done it many times before.

"I can't be seen with the guests," Gideon replied, dropping to a crouch, promptly vanishing behind a bush.

Meredith stared at the place where he was hiding. For some reason, she could feel herself beginning to fall apart again. At times, kindness could be more cruel than the strike of a hand, and she could not think of why.

Mrs. Gourd returned with the tea things, not looking at

Meredith as she arranged them on the worn table. Meredith made sure not to thank her.

When the door closed behind the housekeeper, Gideon popped out of his hiding spot, hat under his arm. He watched her with apprehension, as if fearing that during the intermission she might have changed her mind about offering him tea.

Meredith managed a smile. "If you had brought another chair, I would offer it to you," she said. "And I'm afraid that she only brought one teacup. There are plenty of biscuits, though…"

Gideon shrugged his shoulders, retaking the spot opposite her at the table. "A biscuit and good company, far better than black tea."

She pushed the plate of biscuits across the table where he could reach them. "You consider a Mermaid to be good company, sir?"

The question slipped from her lips—it had been a strange thing to hear, having been told all of her life that her heritage made her a worthless abomination. It was stranger, to her, than the thought of Gideon having returned for no reason except to say hello.

"Don't call me *sir*," Gideon said smilingly. "I'm far from a gentleman. My friends at the pub have sailors' mouths—the ones that don't have four legs, anyway."

Meredith sipped from a glass of salt water, peering at him. It was true: He did not have the polished appearance to which she was accustomed in men. A lifetime of work gave him tired eyes; a dusting of stubble on his face was proof that he had no time to loiter.

The stubble on his face was odd to her—odd because no respectable man in her past would have presented himself without shaving. She glanced away, puzzled that such a small thing should catch her interest.

"You have pets, then?" she inquired.

"I train Grumbacher's dogs," he said. "I look after his horses, too. Poor devils—one of the mares was born with one eye. I suppose it was a mercy that he adopted her before she could be slaughtered as a foal. She's the gentlest of them all."

"I can't imagine living with only one eye," Meredith confessed, watching as he ate a biscuit with large, hungry bites. "Then again..." She did not finish her sentence out loud: *Then again, you could not imagine having fish scales on your skin.*

"It won't be unusual to her," Gideon said in between bites, "as she's never known anything different."

Meredith took the smallest biscuit from the plate—he clearly needed the food more than she did. "Perhaps I could meet her," she said, hearing her own uncertainty as she made a request of him. "If I'm to rot away in this place, it might be enjoyable to go riding."

"Josie would love a visitor," Gideon agreed, reaching for another biscuit—absentmindedly, as though he did not realize what his hand was doing. How long had it been since his last meal? "She turned her nose up at me today. I think horses tire of the same old guests."

She drank more water, recognizing that she stood on an odd balance. In part, she felt uncomfortable confiding in a stranger—confiding in anybody at all. Simultaneously, her soul rejoiced in chat to break the monotony. If only she could stop herself from sneaking glances at him over her glass.

"You said you have friends at a pub," she said. "Does that mean there is civilization nearby?"

He shrugged again. "It's a ways off on foot, and I can only go on my half-days. Horseback will get you there in thirty minutes. Rhys Ellis, the village's called; it's where I used to live with my mother."

"Used to?" Meredith repeated, knowing well that she was being nosy—knowing and not caring. He appeared eager to answer questions as she was to ask them.

"Mum…" He trailed off, momentarily forgetting about the tray of food in front of him. "Something happened when I was very little. No one told me exactly what. She was sent to an asylum in London…by Grumbacher."

Even as sympathy gripped her heart, Meredith was struck by the similarities in their pasts. She did not have a mother, either, and though Lady Adeline Bannister had died, was it much better to have a mother locked away?

"I'm sorry to hear it," she told him. Though she knew condolences provided scant relief, it did not feel right to hear of such a thing and not react.

Gideon's face fell. It was the first time since meeting him that she had seen him anything other than cheerful. "I searched for her once," he confessed. "There are no records about which asylum he sent her to."

Meredith reached for a cloth napkin, wiping her hands though they were clean. "Bannister never told me where my mother was buried, either."

Gideon lifted his chin, replying with a half-smile that caused her heart to skip a beat. "Aren't we lucky with our relations, My Lady?"

She shook her head. "I have never been lucky with anything."

He pondered her response. She was glad that there was no pity in his expression. Pity, sympathy, condolences would not save her from the pit in which she had been abandoned. What she needed was banter; what she needed was to see his half-smile again, though she didn't understand why…

Gideon reached into his pocket and retrieved from it a deck of cards, tied together with a fraying blue ribbon. "Fancy a game?" he asked, untying the knot and spreading the deck on the table.

Meredith smiled at the state of the cards. "They are well loved," she remarked, touching one; so often had they been shuffled that the edges had begun to fray.

"A Christmas present from Mum," Gideon confessed. "The year before she was taken. I call it my lucky deck; when I use it at the pub, I always win."

A knot formed in Meredith's throat. "It might be that she is helping you win," she said, watching him separate the cards into two decks. "Not this time, though. I'm bored enough that a blessing won't save you."

Her chiding words were rewarded once more with that half-smile. "We shall have to give it a try," he said, nudging one of the decks across the table at her. "Let's play for the last biscuit."

Meredith nodded, though she would have given him the biscuit, anyway. "Thank you," she heard herself say. "It —it's exhausting to hear nothing but the voice in my head."

"Believe me, Lady Meredith," Gideon said, sobering. "No one knows that feeling better than me. I live in a garden shed and see people once a week."

They began their game, abandoning their somber

conversation topics, choosing instead to focus on their struggle for the final biscuit.

When Gideon won the first round, Meredith enjoyed the sight of his half-smile, as if she had been the victor.

Fifteen

PETER HAD FORGOTTEN ALL ABOUT JIMMY.

He had only been at the orphanage for two days and was dazzled by Rose's presence. Nothing mattered to him but enjoying sweet moments with her.

When the watchman dropped in for a visit after dinner on the second day, Peter was jolted back to reality. He needed to stay in the watchman's good graces.

Jimmy accepted a seat in one of the mismatched armchairs, balancing in his hand a chipped teacup Marie had offered him. Dark rings under his eyes denoted tiredness; Peter wondered if the man slept, or if he spent every free moment on watch.

"I've got to say," said Jimmy to Peter, "I'm surprised to see you so cheery in a place like this." He shot a pointed glance at Rose, who was busy arranging doilies.

Peter wondered if Jimmy could see the truth: Any happiness he felt in this district was due to her presence, her rare laughter, the clarity in her turquoise eyes. These details gave Peter a lightness he never felt with Meredith.

Was it was too soon to call the lightness love? If he hadn't been in love before, could it be that he basked in the beginnings of it? Rose constantly slipped from his grasp like a beautiful dream; he could not fathom leaving without her.

Jimmy might have been able to guess all of this—he was a man, after all—but it wasn't the sort of thing Peter would confide to him.

"It must be the sea air," Peter said, taking the chair next to Rose. "I can breathe in this place."

"Ironic," said Jimmy. "You might feel that way because you have the liberty to leave." His frank words quickly darkened the mood.

Peter bided his time, accepting a cup of tea from Marie. The redhead seemed determined to sit in for the conversation; once certain that everyone had their tea, she retreated to a corner and listened.

Peter felt that she and the other girls overestimated his importance. They hung on his every word as if hoping for a quote worthy of a storybook. If Peter's life was a fairy tale, he was the cowardly prince who had fled from a damsel.

"Forgive my ignorance," Peter said, staring into his tea. "My father being who he was, I ought to have paid attention. What happens if one of you escapes?"

"Depends," Jimmy said gruffly. "Some of us have scales that are easily hidden with clever clothes. Those are the Mer who most often attempt to leave. Not all are so fortunate; my wife has scales on her right cheek."

He motioned to a spot on his own cheek, as if feeling the mark on his wife's body. After years together, perhaps they were linked.

"My wife could never leave this place; it would be suspicious if she covered her face with a scarf all day. I have never contemplated an escape; I won't live without her."

Peter nodded, solemnly. "Those who leave—where do they go?"

"We have ways. People know people who know people. A Mer who slips out must be scrupulous, never engaging with the wrong person."

Jimmy set his teacup on the table, exhaling.

"If caught, the lucky ones are brought back. If blamed for something like theft or murder, many disappear. I suspect that one of my friends has been locked away for seventeen years. Sorley." His eyes glazed over when he pronounced his friend's name.

"I'm sorry to hear that," Peter mumbled.

Jimmy cleared his throat of emotion before continuing. "In cases when police do not wish to maintain us, hanging is not out of the question. There is never a trial."

Peter felt his blood boil. Hanged—without a trial. Hanged for no reason except to be rid of the Merpeople and their descendants.

A person like Jimmy would be hanged, simply for existing.

A person like Rose.

I must try, though, he thought, looking at Rose. *I've got money and a title. Surely they are worth something.*

Rose's eyes were sad as she looked back at him. *See?* they appeared to tell him. *This is what you ask of me.*

Peter understood—but would not be deterred. He could not, would not, leave her in this wretched place.

They sipped their tea in silence, the conversation having taken a lamentable turn that discouraged banter. After about five minutes, it was Jimmy who broke the silence.

"Well," he said, getting to his feet, "I'd best be off. I'm not done with the watch, and wouldn't want to miss the culprit if he comes by. Thank you for the tea, ladies—and thanks for the conversation, Lord Everly."

Peter nodded; he could not form words.

After Jimmy left, Peter sat with Rose and Marie in silence. He met their eyes and felt small indeed. He could come and go as he pleased; they dared not. He knew of the outside world; for them to see it would mean great danger.

Something needed to change. For the first time, he understood his late father's urgency to advocate for the Mer. Until then, it had been dormant; now he could not put it away.

"If I could change things," he began—but stopped at that, because what could he say? How could he change the hearts of an entire kingdom?

It was Marie who responded from the shadowy corner in which she sat. "You could, My Lord," she said. "You could."

"*To whom it may concern...*" Peter stared at the sheet of paper, at a loss.

He sat in the kitchen alone, Rose having started needle-work with the girls in the sitting room.

There were many' letters he needed to write. He was determined to contact the detectives his father had hired, the ones who failed at their job.

He stared at his signet ring. What good was it being the son of someone great if he did not know how to follow up on something important? It would be easier if he could meet them in person. He would like to know if they had avoided this district on purpose. Such things could be lied about on paper, but body language betrayed everyone.

Rose's voice broke into his thoughts. "Don't forget posture, Lily. It will help you work for longer periods."

He smiled. Rose trained the orphans to behave like ladies, though she had no reason to believe they would be offered better work. She took her time to correct them for the sake of their own dignity.

It made difficult the task of convincing her to leave. How was he to change her life if she so loved her work? By tearing her away, would he not break her heart?

An idea crept over him. He knew how to change her heart without shattering it, but could not do so alone. Mrs. Whittle might give him the advice he needed.

Forgetting about the detectives, he reached for a fresh sheet of paper.

Mother, he wrote…but stopped.

What could he say to Countess Emma that would satisfy her? Was she worried about his disappearance, or angry that he ruined an important day?

Forgive me for not telling you where I am,

he wrote, choosing words that balanced truth and dignity.

I found safety at the end of the world, in a place that is not safe. I've grown tired of being the focus of everyone.

When I told Meredith I would not marry her...

Peter faltered. It was not easy to write what happened, no easier than to speak of it. He did not want to be a coward by blaming his woes on a woman, but was it not the truth? Finding himself in this remote place, he had seen the chaos that resulted from living a life of lies. Father would not have wanted him to lie.

He added a strange sentence to a letter that already sounded ridiculous.

I have found Lady Rose. I've chosen to stay where she is until the time is right.

Peter closed his eyes, accepting that he would not be able to finish his letters tonight. Folding both sheets, he resolved to try again later.

He stood and peered through the kitchen door. Rose was on her knees next to Anne. Her eyes shone as she demonstrated a stitch.

She was happy as a teacher. Though he wished to move her someplace safer, he would not take this pastime away. He would invest in it.

❧

"A LARGER SCHOOL?" Mrs. Whittle repeated. "You would do that for a handful of girls you've known for two days?"

"Perhaps I have not known them for long," he said, watching her wash dishes, "but I've known Rose all my life."

The matron had joined him shortly after his letter-writing efforts. Peter asked her for advice regarding his idea, not wishing to lose his nerve. It was an abrupt change he offered, considering the short time she had known him.

Peter and Mrs. Whittle shared the desire to see Rose happy. They both realized his idea was the only way to convince her out.

"I will risk it, Mrs. Whittle," he said. "I'll buy a house where they will all be safe." *Especially Rose.*

Mrs. Whittle smiled, reaching for a cloth to dry her hands. "I knew you had a good heart. It will be quiet without them, but who am I to deny them a better life?"

If any part of the idea grieved her, she did not let emotion slip through her calm. He knew that she meant what she said; she wished for her girls to be happy.

"You can come, too," he said softly.

"No, sir. I have no desire to leave my house. Unlike Lady Rose, I was born here and have never known anything different. Would you like some tea?"

He nodded and watched her fill two cups. Standing, Peter drew the second chair so that Mrs. Whittle could sit across from him.

She accepted his aid with a tired smile, a sigh of fatigue. The environment became conspiratorial. They were not only discussing Rose's safety; all of the girls deserved a better life.

"My suggestion is that the older pupils be taken as workers, not students," said Mrs. Whittle. "Marie and Isabel have long finished their lessons. They know enough to help with the tasks Rose insists on doing herself."

Peter remembered seeing Marie hanging clothes to dry earlier.

"I agree," he said. "I see no reason why they should be limited because of their heritage. Their behavior is so perfect that I would not have been able to tell them apart in a crowd of…*good company.*" Peter hated to use the term, but frankness was necessary.

Mrs. Whittle beamed. "I hope that, one day, they can marry whomever they want. If the world could see that they're not savages, there would be nothing to stop them."

Peter battled a storm of emotions when he replied. "Shouldn't one marry a person who is kind? Breeding has little to do with it."

You are a fool. Meredith's words would never vanish from his mind, nor would her violence. She had been the coveted lady of the season, the best-bred of them all. Despite this, it was a stroke of luck that he evaded death at her feet. Meanwhile, the kindest woman he knew taught orphans in a place no one wished to visit.

Mrs. Whittle's eyes softened. "There is a haunt in the way you speak. I want you to know that whatever harmed you did not make you a broken man. There is goodness in every word you say."

Peter bowed his head as sadness crept over him. When had Mother ceased to speak tender words like those Mrs. Whittle gave freely?

Marie knocked at the door before leaning in. "I hate to interrupt whatever you two are planning, but *Lady Rose* has asked if *Lord Peter* would like to help with the music." She pronounced the titles with relish.

"Excuse me," he said to Mrs. Whittle. "I told her I would help."

144

"I will join you when I have washed these cups," she said. "I've been told that your playing is good."

Peter hoped that his cheeks were not pink. Rose had been talking about him! He wondered what else she told her friends when he was not around.

He stepped into the drawing room, watching Rose dust off a standing piano. Behind her, the orphans curtsied, drawing her attention to him.

"I hope you aren't too tired," she said. "Or it can be tomorrow."

"Now is fine," he said. Even if he had been exhausted, he would never break his promise.

"Give it a go, then," Rose said. "You will see that it is out of tune."

Peter went to the piano, determined to wring music out of it and bring a smile to her face.

Sixteen

ROSE LISTENED AS PETER TESTED THE PIANO.

There was something alarming in the way he'd looked at her—a resolution, a promise. The man was planning something. Gone was the battered patient who had fallen off of a steed. Before her sat a gallant hero, brave like those in fairy stories.

There was no escaping it: Rose would be a part of his story. Fate had dropped him at her door, marking the first chapter.

What were the chances that, of all people, Peter West should be the wounded man she nursed to health that night? How could it be a coincidence that they found one another in such a manner?

Peter finished testing the piano and began to play a song. She closed her eyes to listen. It was familiar, though she could not recall the title. It pulled her from the crowded room in Mrs. Whittle's orphanage, back into a memory.

She was in Father's music room, underneath the chandelier. The ceiling was high, the velvet curtains pulled aside so that precious sunlight spilled through five bay windows.

Rose watched her mother practice ballet, amazed by the woman's ability to stand on her toes without wincing. On days when no one came to visit, Countless Arabella indulged in her childhood hobby—pirouettes, pliés, graceful leaps. She danced with no music, the songs written into her heart.

Arabella's wedding ring glinted in the light as she raised her hands. It was the ring she gave to Rose after becoming ill, convinced that her daughter might one day need it.

"Sell it," Mother wheezed to Rose, in her final hours. "It is the only dowry I can give you."

Rose had not sold the ring and did not think she ever could.

Peter's song stirred memories she'd buried in her mind, a place where they could not hurt her. The song brought her a deep longing for the countryside, for bright afternoons of ballet and love.

She longed for the safety of Father's house.

Peter finished the song and, after a pause, began another. It was vivid with the freedom of improvisation. It brought to Rose's mind images of stars on cloudless nights. She smelled trees, her mother's perfume, her father's library.

Two notes, poignant and simple—*twinkle*. Two more —*flash*. A chord—light stretching from the full moon looking at the people below.

For the first time in Rose's memory, none of the orphans made a fuss, ensorcelled by the song. She understood, as she was also tangled in the spell.

When Peter reached the final note, Rose had been so immersed in his dream that she could not remember how to speak. With music, he placed at her feet the past. He also offered a future. She knew it was the same future that she had refused earlier.

Rose sensed that, from that moment onward, it would be difficult to tell him no.

When his performance ended, they began vocal lessons. Peter played scraps of song in accompaniment to the girls' voices. Rose struggled to remember she was teaching, not sitting in a concert hall.

The class was brief. Soon, Mrs. Whittle and Marie herded the girls up to bed. Rose knew she had been left alone with Peter intentionally.

She had promised not to slip away from Peter again. Instead, she tried to compose herself while he had his back turned; he hadn't yet left the piano. He was caught, it seemed, on the remainder of a dream. She listened to him tap gentle notes—stars conversing? Crickets chirping? Butterflies in flight? The trail of song invited her to explore his thoughts further.

"You outdid yourself," Rose said, when at last he closed the lid over the keys. "I feel as if I ought to pay you."

"Don't be silly."

"You should not give your talent for free."

"It isn't free," he said, turning. "Your company is worth every song."

Rose could not think of a response. Instead, she managed a smile, wondering if a blush had crept up her cheeks.

Peter stood. He wore the dazed look of a person caught in mid-flight.

"To be fair, I have never charged anyone to hear music,"

he said. "It wouldn't be a true escape if trapped in the cage of currency."

Rose felt a sudden longing to close the distance between them. She wanted to tell him that, for a few seconds, he had taken her home. She wanted to thank him for the reminder of Mother's beauty and the warmth of country life.

"You know what you've done," Rose whispered.

Peter had complete mastery over the keys, even those of an out-of-tune piano. Like a wizard, he had chosen each note to cast a spell.

He took a step forward—a tantalizing step. "Did it work?"

Come closer, said her heart, though Rose did not know what she would do if he did.

"It might have," she answered. "I can't tell you yet."

"That's progress," he said, eyes shining.

Rose looked away. She remained in the bliss cast by those songs, but something else set in. She wrestled with the sense that basking in her memories was a form of betrayal.

This orphanage saved her life, but did she ever promise *not* to leave? If she returned to the country, she would miss the ocean air. However, the music stirred memories of grassy fields, forests, and wildflowers.

"I wish it was simple," she whispered. "I fear that I have become two people."

"You don't have to give up either of them," he said. "It's possible to love two places at once."

Rose wondered if *he* could love a person who was in two places.

How could she wish for him to come nearer, if not for this emotion so like those described in love poems? How could she ask it of him, when she could not decide which part of her was most important?

"You *are* stubborn," she said with a nervous laugh.

To which he replied, "You're worth it."

Peter did not close the distance. It must have been Rose's fault for marking the space between them so well. She raised her guard, forbidding him from calling her the name he remembered her by. It fell on her, then, to make amends.

Rose mustered the courage to step forward, but knew not what to say. Words did not exist to describe the change in her heart.

"That woman who hurt you made a mistake," she said. "I hope you will see your great worth."

Peter became still. Rose watched him grapple with a dark emotion that had been hanging over him since his reappearance. "Thank you," he said. "I needed to hear that."

Choose now, she thought. *He deserves to be fought for.*

If Rose had been braver, she might have walked into his arms. She might have given in and touched him, inhaled his scent whilst they were alone.

She did none of these things.

Rose had become fearful and weak. She did not deserve to have him in front of her, waiting for words that would bring him comfort.

"I should go to bed," she whispered. Then, a question tumbled from her heart: "Will you be here in the morning?"

Her heart must have feared the consequences of her cowardice. Instead of touching him, she had chosen to walk off. She knew her continued distance hurt him, though he did not say so.

Peter nodded. "And the next."

Relief flooded through her. "Good night, then. And thank you."

Peter inclined his head in response.

In the dim light of the lamp, she was struck by how handsome he had become. It was no wonder the girls were fascinated by him. He had a smile that would linger in any woman's memory.

Rose curtsied, turning away before his smile could distract her. She made a beeline for the stairs, not looking over her shoulder, lest his quiet charm capture her again.

Entering the bedroom, she closed the door, leaning against it. Silent tears leaked down her cheeks. Her heart wrestled with too many emotions for one evening—too many for one person.

Though awake, Marie did not ask about the tears, pretending to be immersed in a book.

As Rose changed into her nightdress, she realized that her tears were not of sadness, but love.

Seventeen

MEREDITH PACED. SHE HAD GONE IN SO MANY CIRCLES THAT she suspected she would make a mark on the wooden floor. A weak hearth flickered; she searched the crackling sound for words, a ghost to break the silence.

Grumbacher House was empty. The servants seemed to avoid her part of the mansion; she did not even have their footsteps to break the monotony. A selection of books waited on a shelf for her perusal, but she could not settle her mind to focus on literature.

Silence was crippling.

Loneliness, crippling.

Sighing, she turned to stare into the fireplace; it seemed to share in her despair. It moved about as best it could in hopes of attention.

Meredith considered going to bed, but was not tired. She sat in one of the armchairs, staring at her hands, wondering if it would be freedom to disappear—like the hearth would eventually do.

She was startled by the sound of a pebble hitting the

window. Meredith scrambled to her feet, but found herself rooted to the spot, unable to drag herself to a hiding spot.

Another pebble.

"My Lady!" someone called through the open window. It took her a ridiculous minute to realize that the voice belonged to Gideon.

Trembling, she pushed aside the curtain and leaned out. He had climbed a tree outside of the window; in the darkness, she could see a sack slung over his shoulder.

"You're insane," she hissed. "Climbing a tree! Couldn't you—"

"I can't well get through the front door," Gideon reasoned. "Here."

He held out the sack. Meredith stared at it with confusion before accepting the offering. Opening it, she found bits of candy wrapped in colorful paper.

"Where did this come from?" she asked, her voice thickening, though she could not name the emotion that she felt.

"I went down to the village," he said. "Played some card games for candy. You can hardly expect me to eat it all on my own."

A knot formed in her throat. She looked at him once more, sitting precariously on a branch, and tried to make a quick decision. It would not be kind to leave him there like an overgrown sparrow, but inviting him in would be wildly inappropriate.

Or it would have been, if anybody in the mansion existed who cared whether she was dead or alive.

"That branch is going to break," she said, clearing her throat. "Normal people don't make visits on treetops."

She saw him blink, surprised by her implied invitation. "Sure I won't be interrupting anything?"

"There's absolutely nothing here for you to interrupt," Meredith said, and she heard her desperation. *Please come inside,* said her heart. *Talk about the pub. Give me something to listen to.*

Gideon seemed to sense her plea. "All right," he said, "if you share the candy."

He gripped the windowsill and hauled himself through with great ease—she imagined it was the product of a life of manual work. Meredith felt her knees weaken. It was not the moment to cry, but she found it easier to be strong when there was no one to see her. Interaction, it pierced her to the core.

The words spilled from her mouth: "I'm in shock that you came."

Gideon took the bag of candy and emptied the contents onto the carpet. Helping her to sit on the ground, he huddled up beside her, and they were for a moment quiet, breathing in the sweet scent of candy.

"I thought you would send me off, honest," he admitted, sorting the blue candies into a pile. "Where you're from, my presence at night would raise more than one eyebrow. The truth is…" He shrugged his shoulders. "I've had the candy for some time, but no one to share it with, and—and could do with some conversation. It gets lonely, you know. I live in a garden shed. Hours of no sound but the wind on the plains."

He offered her a candy wrapped in red paper, which she accepted. How great must be his loneliness; this had been his prison for a lifetime, and she was struggling to adjust with the silence after only five days.

"I've never had a person to talk to, either," she admitted, "unless my ladies' maid counts. She was paid to stay by my side. I'm not convinced she was always willing to hear me bemoan my life."

Gideon unwrapped a bit of taffy, eating with a distant look on his face. Meredith watched him while his face was turned. He was an odd mix of boyishness with the sobering pain of adulthood. He could jest and make her laugh at his own expense, but a sadness remained in the downward tilt of his lips.

"My name is Greer," he told her. "Gideon Greer. I changed it. I refuse to have that man's surname, whether he'd like to give it to me or not."

"Why did you choose Greer?"

"A shortened version of his name. I don't know if it was a creative choice, but I can live with being Greer."

Meredith felt a curious urge to touch his hand. It went against everything she had taught herself about interacting with men—namely, that she should feel nothing for them, neither love nor sympathy. That had been a rule to safeguard her heart for the day when she would be given away.

Perhaps now that Bannister tossed her out, she had lost the energy to maintain such barriers. Perhaps it was the fact of Gideon being a kindred spirit; his pain was not unlike hers. They had more in common than seemed possible.

"You don't deserve to be here," he said, "in a place where no one can see you. I don't understand…"

"I'm a Mermaid, Mr. Greer," she said, tired. "For many, including Lord Bannister, that is more than enough of a reason to send me out and forget me."

"It won't work, though," he argued. "You're not forgettable. You're beautiful."

Meredith smiled, struck by his words. "You're only saying that because I'm the only woman within miles."

"No," he said, frustrated, "that's not it. I didn't forget you. I recognized you when you arrived, even though you had grown older. You aren't forgettable, and maybe you don't want to live in a world where people will be deliberately blind to that. They don't deserve your presence."

She sorted through the candies, making patterns of bright color. "I suppose that's one perspective. Thank you for being kind to me."

Her voice broke; tears slid down her face, blurring the candy on the carpet, and sobs rattled her body. *Alone, alone, alone*—the word repeated in her mind like a drum, throbbing along with every sob, and her chest hurt from trying without success to keep her misery in check, like it had always been.

Gideon caught her.

It was with uncertainty that he first held her, perhaps expecting that she would shove him away—after all, such close contact was close to scandal, and pressed her to him as if doing so would keep her from dissolving until pieces.

He didn't tell her to stop crying; it wouldn't have done any good. He might have sensed that her tears came from years of forced silence and untruth.

When his chest heaved, Meredith thought that he might have been crying, as well—but she did not open her eyes to see, giving him the dignity of privacy.

"One day," he breathed into her ear—chills, the sensation of his breath brought her chills—"one day, that world will come to its senses. It will realize that you no longer grace its halls, that your smile no longer gives it color, and your laughter doesn't break the silence. Those people will miss you, but it'll be too late. I know that you can find a place of your own, and you can build your own happiness."

"But I d—don't deserve to—to be happy," she hiccoughed. "I'm a M—Mermaid."

His grip did not loosen; her tears did not slow. "I'm holding you, and you are a woman. And I might be dirt-poor, but now I am the luckiest man in the world, because I am holding you and no one else is."

He drew an old handkerchief from his jacket and wiped the tears from her face, though more kept coming. Seventeen years worth of sadness could not be absorbed with one cloth. Meredith could only hope that he was saying the truth.

He knew what she was, but saw her as a woman.

The truth hit her like a spear: In her mind, throughout her life, she had only been a Mermaid.

Judging by the way he held her, perhaps she was not only a woman, but also a beautiful one.

Eighteen

EVEN WHILE TRAPPED IN GRUMBACHER HOUSE, NUMBNESS was possible.

Meredith cursed each endless day. A week had passed since her arrival, though she did not realize it until Agnes brought breakfast on the seventh day.

Mail had been stacked on the tray, next to her plate—an elegant envelope and, under it, a folded bit of paper.

Jarred from her state of nonexistence, she broke the wax seal on the envelope. To her chagrin, she saw it was from Grumbacher. Instead of using her proper name, he used the title she could never escape.

Mermaid,

I have decided to visit today. Expect me in the afternoon. You can tell me how you find the *place and whether anything can be changed for your comfort.*

—G

"IT WAS KIND OF him to warn me," Meredith said with sarcasm, tossing the envelope aside.

She reached for the folded paper. The missive had an air of afterthought. It was not real mail, but a message that had been cleverly hidden.

Gideon, she thought. No one else in this place would have taken the time to do such a thing.

Wondering what he had taken such great lengths to say, she unfolded the paper.

Lady Meredith, it read—his handwriting clumsy but legible—

I'm sure the letter on this tray will tell you of the homeowner's visit. He can't know we're acquainted. I'm not supposed to talk to guests.

I will be working as a footman. Pretend we never met. I can't protect you if he sends me away. Hide this note.

Yours,

G. Greer

Her eyes lingered on the word *protect.* No one ever tried to protect her, certainly not her 'father'. Lord Bannister raised her to make him look sophisticated, tossing her away when she ceased to be useful.

"Agnes," she said, folding the note until it was a square in the palm of her hand, "dress me so I won't look frightened. I'll wear red today."

Agnes sorted through the wardrobe, silent as always.

The day before, she had not acted with surprise when Meredith used her name. Rather, she seemed relieved that someone secured her identity without forcing her to speak.

Meredith placed Gideon's note inside of her pillowcase. She then stood, bracing herself for a long day.

Gideon must have a reason for his alarmed reaction. Meredith would trust that he knew this place better than she did. If he wanted to protect her, she would let him.

On a normal day, Meredith would have gone to her table on the veranda. Gideon would appear with the post, and they would chat to pass the time.

It was not possible to slip out now.

After Agnes finished with her hair, Meredith found herself alone in her rooms. She fidgeted, pacing in front of her fireplace. The hearth had not been lit, it being a warm day.

Her gaze trailed to the door.

Protect you, Gideon wrote.

Meredith swallowed. Though she had not come for a conventional marriage, she wondered what he knew about Grumbacher to make him use that word.

Protect.

A memory struck her.

After Grumbacher agreed to take Meredith, he and Bannister exchanged correspondence. Meredith stumbled across the letters on Bannister's desk one night. She had visited the library in search of a book. Instead, she found images that would give her nightmares.

Grumbacher sent Bannister dozens of diagrams, sketches of Merpeople sliced like cattle. The most grisly depicted bones. Meredith remembered wondering which unfortunate Mermaid had been cut open. How else could their bones be revealed?

Now alone in Grumbacher's house, Meredith felt fear in the pit of her stomach. Rather than freeze her, it egged her on. She slipped into the corridor, casting a glance downstairs. The housekeeper was busy ensuring that a tidy house awaited the master's return.

No one heard Meredith walk to the forbidden wing, using her skill of soundlessness. No one saw her try the doorknob. It gave with surprising ease, as if someone had been expecting her.

You will regret having gone. Grumbacher's ominous words repeated in her memory as she pushed the door in.

It was dark in this part of the mansion—dark and oddly cold.

Meredith stepped inside, closing the door behind her. "I will not regret being aware," she whispered.

Her vision focused. The windows had been boarded up, allowing a sliver of light. By the door, armchairs were covered with sheets. Cupboards lined the far wall; across from them, a corridor stretched into shadow.

Meredith chose not to look into that blackness. Instead

she made for the cupboards, treading lightly so that the servants would not hear. She did not want anyone to know she had ventured into the forbidden wing.

She opened a cupboard to reveal shelves of illustrations. Taking one, she held it to the light. It depicted a Mermaid from the waist down. Its focus appeared to be on the pattern of her scales. The artist paid remarkable attention to detail; Meredith almost touched the page, expecting to feel texture.

She replaced the drawing, shifting her attention to a pile of journals. It was tempting to open one and read, but she knew that doing so would rob her of the little sleep she already managed.

Spotting a drawer, she reached for the knob, fingers trembling. Then, she heard footsteps in the corridor behind her.

Meredith dared not look over her shoulder. She turned on her heel and made a swift exit, closing the door with silence despite her uneven breathing.

You will regret it, Grumbacher said.

Meredith returned to her quarters. She dropped into an armchair by the fireplace, rubbing her sweaty palms on her skirt.

Why? she thought, closing her eyes. *Why did I do it? Who saw me?*

She tried to regain her composure in time to greet Grumbacher with dignity. It was difficult, for all of a sudden she imagined a new drawing in the cupboard.

It was a drawing of her.

If someone in the forbidden wing intended to harm her, why wait? Would they not have found a way to capture her by now? Ignored as she was in a corner of the mansion, it seemed unlikely that they cared to slice her open.

Yet she had been brought for a purpose. Lord Bannister arranged for her to be a part of this collection. Not once had he disguised his intentions of being rid of her.

Gideon's words about Agnes stirred Meredith's panic. *I'm not certain that she can't speak,* he told her. *I suspect that she won't.*

What could have happened to Agnes that was awful enough to steal her voice? Meredith determined to learn the truth about the maid as soon as possible.

It was not fair that she should continue to be treated like a chair. Meredith was not a piece of furniture to cover with a sheet. She would not accept it anymore.

Meredith vowed to learn the plans they had for her. She would not be robbed of the chance to leave the world with courage.

Nineteen

One week after writing his letters, Peter felt no urgency to send them. He did not want to break his anonymity. He did not wish to alert the world that he was alive. They remained on his bedside table, unsealed.

Peter knew his song had evoked emotions in Rose that startled her. It wasn't his intention to cause her unease, but to touch the young girl she had been.

After his performance, he feared she would turn away from him for being intrusive. Instead, she greeted him with a smile the following morning. Reassured by this, Peter changed his plan.

Stifling his impatience to rescue her, he chose to become a part of her life. Instead of pressuring her to leave, he found himself sitting at the kitchen table seven days later, keeping Rose company while she made bread.

Mrs. Whittle had given him a notebook to pass the time. He filled empty moments, sketching with a stubby pencil, jotting thoughts and observations. Once back in proper society, he would use the notes to proceed with his orphanage.

Peter finished a loose sketch of a landscape while Rose kneaded dough. She focused on the task at hand, not venturing into small talk. When at last she broke her silence, she seemed to be thinking out loud.

"There won't be lessons today. It's too warm to stay in the house."

"You're inside," he pointed out, adding shadow to his landscape. "Making bread—at an oven. Shouldn't you have a break, too?"

Rose flashed a smile that distracted him more than it should have. "I will go outside later. I don't fancy not doing anything."

She paused to wipe her hands on a cloth. Peter turned back to his drawing before she could notice his stare.

"How is Sybil?" Rose asked. "I have been wondering about her."

Peter set his pencil aside. Was it progress that Rose had asked about *the outside world* unprompted? Careful not to reach conclusions, he answered her question.

"She's…not a disappointment," he said. "Everyone wants to dance with her, and she enjoys attention. We couldn't be more different."

"Don't make it sound so grim," she said. "If you had been given the chance to make choices, you would enjoy attention, too."

"I doubt it," he said. "People like me don't have the luxury of choice, no matter what others think. At some point, I am expected to oversee the trading business."

"Who manages it now?"

"My uncle Theo. He has experience with it, and offered

to manage it for me while…" He trailed off, not wishing to speak of Meredith or the mockery of an engagement.

But Rose smiled, the tilt of her head encouraging him to go on. He knew she would not ask more questions if he changed the subject. She deserved to know of his past; after all, she had shown him hers.

"My uncle is clever with numbers." Walking past her, he peered out the window into the garden. "He was helping before Father died. It wasn't much of a challenge for him to become steward. It's not his responsibility, though; eventually, I have to show interest."

"It was kind of him to take the burden," Rose said, opening a cupboard. "It would have been kinder if he had talked to you. He might have realized you were not well."

"Yes," he mumbled. "It might have been simpler if I was open about it."

Rose did not comment on this. Instead she said, "It *is* warm here. Will you open the window?"

Glad to change the subject, he pushed aside the glass. A sea breeze floated past the shutters, filling the kitchen. Over the hedge, he spotted a glimpse of the ocean.

The scenery distracted him; he did not notice Rose approaching until she spoke next to him. "This place could be beautiful," she said.

"It is beautiful," Peter admitted. "I wish people lived here voluntarily. It's impossible to ignore that they cannot leave."

"Somehow," Rose said with wonder, "not every moment here is terrible."

As if on cue, two young girls raced across the yard. Their laughter was not forced, but pure. Their hair had come undone in the wind. He could not help but smile at their innocence.

In seconds, he had glimpsed Rose's childhood. Not all of it was terrible, and the epiphany gave him peace.

"Can I help?" he asked, looking at the mound of dough waiting to be baked. "Then you could step out. It's a shame to waste a lovely day."

Rose glanced at the dough. He saw her shoulders relax as she came to a decision. She took a bowl from the cupboard and placed it over the mound.

"Let's go outside," she said. "I can take a moment's stroll."

Their eyes met, and he searched her turquoise gaze. Gone was the apprehension she wrestled with when he arrived, the fear that caused her to lie about her name. In its place was something else. It hinted at the trust he wanted to earn, making it difficult to turn away.

Peter battled an urge to touch a lock of her hair that had gone astray while she worked. He watched the wind tug at it and was jealous. If he dared for a moment to be like the wind, would she flee from him?

"You aren't a failure," Rose said, forcing his attention from the lock of hair. "Perhaps this is the place where you will learn to make your own choices."

He smiled. "I doubt I will learn to run a business."

"That will happen later." She opened the door and stepped into the garden; Peter stumbled after her. "When you get to it, you won't be afraid. When you aren't afraid, you will learn the business and be better at it than your uncle."

"I don't think I can be better than my uncle," he said, taking a breath of sea air. "If he isn't angry with me, we can run it together."

He trailed off, feeling a stab of homesickness—not for

his mother or the house he inherited, but for his uncle's advice.

Uncle Theo guided him after Father's death with great patience, until the engagement distracted Peter from anything that did not involve a perfect match. Uncle Theo never walked away. It was Peter who stopped visiting, stopped talking and asking for advice.

What would his uncle have said if Peter had the confidence to ask for help?

"It appears that the others have gone to that field," Rose said, breaking his reverie. "Let's join them. You can confirm your theory about daisies being the same," she added with a smile.

He reached for her hand, pulling her near enough that he could memorize the angles of her face, the color in her cheeks, the sound of her surprised laugh. She did not pull away. He dared to think she might be happy standing nearer to him.

Remembering his manners, Peter released her with a mumbled apology, waiting for her to back away. She did not. His week of patient silence must have settled a storm.

"I think," he said, "it's an opportunity to have a conversation without eavesdroppers."

"Yes," she whispered. "If you are willing to listen with an open heart, then I am able to talk with one."

In the moment when he'd seen those girls running on the grass, he understood. The dank world he imagined was not all Rose had known. She'd had moments of lightness, too. He would listen and, if necessary, wait another week— or two—or three.

Peter followed her to a bench near the hedge. They sat and listened to the sound of children playing in the distance. He waited, determining it best to let her begin with her feelings.

What she said, though, startled him.

"Do you realize that if you appear with me in *your world*," she said, tone remarkably steady, "our reputations will be forged? We might be expected to marry."

Peter had thought of many outcomes that might follow Rose's appearance. Somehow, marriage hadn't been one of them. The thought of marrying her was not unappealing; what caused him hesitation was the idea that they would be *expected* to.

Rose was right. In *his world,* appearing with her could damage his reputation—and it *would* damage hers, because no one knew where she had been.

She continued. "I don't want to be another obligation. You have good intentions, but cannot escape the pressure of your society. Already you have buckled from it once. I want you to know what it is like to—to be yourself...and make your own choices."

He wanted to speak, afraid that her speech was leading to rejection.

At last she finished: "It's not a simple matter of getting me home. If this is what you want, a plan needs to be made. If you return with me, it might be for the rest of your life... because there is no point in me leaving this place to a world I scarcely remember, if I am destined to be alone."

Twenty

ROSE KNEW HER WORDS WERE HARSH TO THE EARS OF A person damaged by the topic of marriage, but he had stayed for one week, awaiting a response. He deserved an honest one.

She continued in a rush. "I don't have a future worth fighting for there if I am alone. Everyone thinks I'm dead, Peter! What will they assume if I return, all grown up, with no answer as to where I've been? Other people are not kind like you. I'll have nowhere to go. You have money and a title. What have I got?"

"Forgive me." There was sadness in his words; she wondered why it hurt to hear. "I did not think about it."

"I would be surprised if you had thought about marriage since arriving," she said. "You come from a world of cover-ups and feigned perfection. When you return to your house, people might forget with time that you disappeared. What about me? I—I'm dead. I vanished with scandal on my very *name.* I don't think I could even be hired as a chambermaid, unless I changed my identity and…I won't do that."

"You're right," he said quickly. "My priority has been to get you out of here. I was waiting for you to give me an answer before I thickened the plan. Still, I was a fool to not think you wouldn't have your terms."

"It can't be a *term*," Rose protested. "That is something forced, and I care too much to force you. Before I walk back into the fire, I would like...to be respected. People won't respect me, but they can't hurt me unless I'm on my own—"

"I never said you would be on your own," he cut in. "Never!"

Rose loathed herself for having forced him to look at the fine points of his dream. It would be easy to follow him if she was a different person, but she did not have the stomach to change her name. It would imply shame, something she never felt about her lineage.

What was it that caused her to say such things? Was it pride, the ghost of Lady Rose asserting her dignity? Was it fear at the thought that he hadn't left in a week? Did her words come from a place of love?

Looking up, she found herself staring at his frailty. For a fraction she lost sight of the gallant prince who sat at the piano.

Fear darkened his face, and she knew. It was a deep fear of rejection, planted in his heart when Meredith hurt him. The woman left him shattered. He might have learned to put on airs in order to conceal it, but had yet to overcome that fear.

Lady Meredith shattered a good man, simply to prove herself more powerful. Rose would have taken his broken pieces; even they gleamed with peculiar beauty.

She could not reach for him, though, when he had yet to

find himself. She could not force him to make a decision—but neither could he make her leave without protection.

"Your heart is still wounded," she whispered.

He looked up, struck; she continued before he could protest.

"Understand that I love you, Peter. I love you too much to use you for safety or hide behind your title. I love you too much to steal your freedom of choice."

Feeling the sting of defeat, she forced herself to her feet. He also stood, the protest in his eyes not reaching his lips. Rose's speech had taken his voice, but she could not have kept silent any longer. It was time to end his dream that her return could be simple.

"Rose," Peter began, faltering.

"I have to finish the bread," she said. "The others will be returning."

He raised his voice. "Rose, wait!"

She had hoped to vanish before he could see her tears. However, it would not be fair to leave before he could answer.

Holding her breath, she met his eyes. The fire in his expression startled her.

"I am *not* a coward," he whispered. "Not anymore."

The prince was back, his strength somehow greater after she had witnessed his weakness. This man was willing to bash every wall that stood before him, even those he built.

Peter continued. "I might not have thought of marriage, but did you think it would frighten me?"

Rose could not admit that, for a moment, her trust in him failed. He knew she had glimpsed his weakness; she had said enough to strain their friendship.

She did not dare answer. It was his turn to speak.

"Did you think I would run away?" he asked gently. "That I would abandon you for requesting a proper life? Marrying you would be an honor."

Rose listened, exhausted by the emotions in her heart. She knew he was the only soul who would call marrying her an *honor*.

"If you don't wish to come with me, I won't force you," he continued. "I see that your roots here are deep. Understand this, Rose—I might find distraction in business, perhaps I will talk to my family, but if I walked away from you...I would never love again."

Her confusion must have reflected in her expression, for he said in a rush: "I am not confused. Don't write this off as a product of my wound. Tell me yes or no, but don't say I can't understand myself!"

"We were children when I vanished," she stammered. "The rumors you must have heard growing up—that I had died—or perhaps worse—how can you think of this lightly? I did not bring it up without a week of thought. Don't you care what they'll think of you?"

"Hang the rumors, Rose!" he said. "I've spent months caring only for what people think of me. Look what happened! I want to be happy, and this might do the trick." He took a step closer, his expression tense with nerves.

The yard was spacious and fresh, but Rose struggled to take a breath. She had expected him to be discouraged by the idea of marriage. Instead, he placed his heart before her —she could imagine it beating with desperation at her feet.

"Now," Peter continued, "I can't stay if you don't want me to. You won't find it so charming if I'm on the kitchen chair a month from now. I've understood that your choice is more important than my stubbornness. Say the word and I will stay for years. If there is hope for me, I'll wait. If you go with me, I promise you will be happy. You will never be a *chambermaid!*"

The sun poured light generously, making poignant his golden features. He might have been startled by her idea, yet here he was, asking for permission to stay.

She would not insult him by doubting any longer.

Peter took her hand and waited. She laced her fingers through his, choosing to enjoy the comforting touch.

"I'm sorry," she managed, as the severity of her words hit her. "It wasn't ladylike of me to ask what I did."

"It's reasonable, Rose, and I'm grateful that you know your own worth. After all, what I ask of you is no small matter."

A nervous laugh escaped her as she pulled away.

Words had been said and emotions felt, but neither of them could gather themselves enough to make a plan. At least he had not stalked away.

Rose bit her lip, knowing she had turned beet-red. What would Mother have thought of her forwardness?

"Don't go," she whispered, unable to look him in the eye. "I—do want you here."

"You won't be annoyed to see me in the kitchen?"

"Not at all."

The sound of laughter announced the girls' return.

Rose backed away, breathing slowly. The matter of her future was yet to be settled. Asking for marriage was something no lady ought to do. She would not blame Peter if he realized later that it did bother him.

Again he read her mind and said, "I promise, Rose. It's not marriage I'm afraid of."

Before she could inquire about his fear, she heard the

garden gate open. "Look, Rose! Wild strawberries!" Marie called. "We gathered enough for dessert!"

Rose hurried to the kitchen, an unfinished conversation burning behind her. If he was still at the orphanage later, they could talk again.

In the kitchen, Rose pretended to be interested in the strawberries. Marie was so distracted that she did not notice a tear slide down Rose's face.

It was a mercy—for she would be mortified to explain.

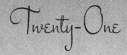

Twenty-One

GRUMBACHER'S VOICE ECHOED IN THE HALL. MEREDITH pressed her ear to the door, holding her breath. He was giving instructions for servants to carry something upstairs.

"Place it in the East Wing," he said. "I will arrange things later."

Her hand rested on the doorknob. She knew that she would provoke a row if she remained hidden. Gideon wrote that she should behave with calm; that might have been possible before her visit to the forbidden room.

Meredith listened to footsteps as Grumbacher's orders were carried out. Something was being delivered to the room she entered earlier.

The only thing she could do was act with poise. It was not for nothing that she was trained to smile through pressure, pretending to be happy, pretending to be confident. Fear wasn't enough to make her forget the role of Lady Meredith.

Once the footsteps were out of earshot, she opened the

door. Lifting her chin, she walked to the landing and peered down.

Grumbacher was dressed flawlessly as usual, talking to the housekeeper. Uncertain of what to do, Meredith pretended to cough.

Catching sight of her, the housekeeper scowled and hurried off. Meredith wondered about Mrs. Gourd's scowl, but maintained her poise.

"Ah," said Silas Grumbacher, taking his hat off. "I wondered if you would come out."

Meredith remained at the top of the stairs, not knowing how to respond. Why did Grumbacher want to see her? She was nothing to him. He had not even married her, when she spent her life preparing to be his wife. She had long begun to tire of his cruel game.

"Join me for tea," he said. It was not a request, she knew, because of the steel in his tone.

Meredith descended. *He will not see my fear,* she thought, ignoring the portraits she passed. *If I am to die, I will go bravely.*

"The housekeeper says that you spend time outside," said Grumbacher as she neared him. "So much that you asked for a table."

Meredith bit her tongue, attempted to relax. Mrs. Gourd would have told him that Gideon brought the table, but she had no way of knowing they formed a friendship.

"You said in the letter that I should feel comfortable," she said, managing a level voice. "I can hardly sit on grass."

Grumbacher stared, reading her expression for some evidence of mischief. Meredith did not cringe, well-practiced in the art of the stare. No man who tried to read her eyes succeeded.

His look of frustration told her that he had failed, as well. "You haven't gone to the East Wing."

She managed not to smirk, but only just. He was guessing, grasping at straws, thrown off by her performance.

"No," Meredith said. "I prefer it outside. The plains are lovely, don't you think?" Turning, she pretended to be interested in the view out the window.

Grumbacher ran a hand through his hair. "Come," he said, turning his back on her. "Tea is in the sitting room."

Meredith followed, smiling at his back. She could pretend this was a ball. He was a gentleman trying but failing to garner her attention. With such a ruse, she could end the day without giving him a victory.

She entered the sitting room and took in the decor. It was a pleasant change from the shadowy corridors. Regal paper colored the walls, decorated with landscapes rather than old portraits. No painted eyes followed her movements. Elegant couches of soft yellow provided comfortable seating.

She took a chair by the open window, and Grumbacher sat by the fireplace. Awkwardness set in as they faced one another.

On a table between them waited a tray of tea things. Meredith wondered if she was expected to serve the beverage. When he did so instead, she scowled. It was no more appealing to accept a drink from the man.

"Well," he said, holding out a cup, "is there anything you would like to talk about?"

Meredith stared at his face. It felt rather as though he were laughing at her. Would he answer her inquiries if she made them? Dared she to think that he might be different from Lord Bannister—no better at heart, but without the need to hide behind lies?

She decided to speak. He would not believe her if she pretended no curiosity existed.

"I might have," she said, looking into her fragrant teacup. "Though you will forgive me for wondering if it is worth asking them."

"Why?" Grumbacher asked the question honestly, as though he could not believe she had kept it to herself—that she would live in a place and not have questions.

"Because," she said, "you abandoned me here with my trunks and a warning to avoid a certain wing. There has yet to be a wedding which, though I cannot deny is a relief, puzzles me. My maid is a mute, I have not heard a word from outside, I don't have a newspaper to read. Someone was kind enough to set a table for me, but aside from that I have found no kindness." A lie, to protect Gideon. "I suppose if you want to know, my question is *what do you want from me?*"

Grumbacher's expression changed into a smile. "That's more like it," he said, stirring his tea. "I was promised someone who could hold a conversation, not a fickle girl who wouldn't take notice of things."

Meredith glared. "After I memorized the faces in your horrific paintings, I had little to take notice of except the quiet. Was I supposed to see something specific? You forbade me from visiting a certain wing."

"For some reason, I feel you are omitting things," he said. "That is another matter. You asked a question and I am surprised. I thought Lord Bannister would have told you."

"Lord Bannister told me nothing," she said, unable to keep the anger from her words. "After he brought me the first time, he forgot I had a mind capable of thought. He trained me like a dog to charm gentlemen, dance, and never fall in love. He said nothing about your plans, only that I had no future with another man."

Grumbacher's eyebrows shot up. She saw his displeasure when he said, "Well, well. This complicates things, Meredith."

His sudden use of her Christian name startled her into nearly dropping the teacup; she tightened her grip and took a drink, attempting to gather herself.

"Surely you know *why* you could not have a future with someone else," he chided.

"*Mermaid,*" spat Meredith. "He was tireless in reminding me that my heritage made me unworthy of a good life with a man of my age."

"That's the point," Grumbacher said, indignant. "I have half a mind to write him a letter. I thought he would be helpful. None of this was meant to be a secret from you. Very well, I shall do my best to explain why you are here— and why, to your relief, we aren't married and will not be."

She took another sip, hoping he could not see her shock.

"If I am successful," Grumbacher said, his words surprisingly kind, "you won't have to worry about *Mermaid* anymore. All evidence of it will disappear, and you'll be able to marry whom you wish. There'll be no danger of them seeing anything different."

Meredith's teacup was nearly empty, as was her mind. The things that Grumbacher told her were ridiculous, outlandish, wrong.

"What?" she asked, her voice but a breath.

"I have been searching for years," he said. "Searching and experimenting for a solution to your malady. Recently, an acquaintance of mine discovered a cure. It was written in a Frenchman's journal, washed ashore in the debris of a ship-wreck. By the time we're finished, there won't be a *Mermaid* in you. Only a woman will remain, lovely and fit for Society."

Meredith feared that she might be sick. "You aren't making sense. You're mad."

"No," said Grumbacher with frustration. "To you, I must sound mad, and it is no thanks to Lord Bannister. You will feel better if you finish the tea."

Meredith drained the cup—not because she wanted tea, but she wished to do something other than stare at him in horror.

"Once the Mermaid has died," said Grumbacher, "we can heal other unfortunate souls born with your condition. You will be able to do what you want. I know it is difficult to grasp now, but you'll be happy."

"How," she managed, "how do you plan to—to *kill the Mermaid?*"

"Well," he said, with a glint of malice, "you finished the tea. That was the first step."

"What?"

"It is a treatment, Meredith. The most difficult part is the beginning. The choice, you might say, to initiate. I have removed that burden."

As Grumbacher stood, Meredith felt herself become faint. Pain flared somewhere deep inside. Her head was heavy, but it was not the weight of an ordinary swoon.

"You might want to lie down." He took the teacup from her hands in a mockery of kindness. "Your mother should not have taken the elixir while standing. Though I suspect there was something unusual about how it affected her."

"Mother?" Meredith gasped, unable to keep her head up.

"Don't worry," he said as the world faded. "I have improved the potion since then. It won't kill you. You will be uncomfortable for a few days…"

He might have said more, but blackness took her.

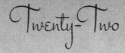

Twenty-Two

PETER WAS DISMAYED TO FIND THAT AWKWARDNESS HAD ONCE more slipped between him and Rose. She scarcely had a word to offer him at dinner.

Astute as she was, Mrs. Whittle must have noticed the change in their interaction. She did not ask about it. Instead she tried to strike up a conversation with him.

"Have you found your stay agreeable, sir?" she asked. "It's been over a week. Surely you've noticed the unbearable heat."

He smiled and said, "It is quite hot."

"I wondered," said Mrs. Whittle, "if you will be staying long enough that more clothes should be obtained for you. Jimmy would be glad to provide them, as he has done before."

Rose had told him earlier that she wished for him to stay. He searched her expression for some indicator that her wish had changed. She offered the tiniest of smiles, reaching for her water.

Interpreting this as reassurance, Peter said, "I will stay for as long as I am welcome."

"Very good," said Mrs. Whittle. "In the morning I will tell him to find you more clothes. There is going to be a play this weekend, at the parish. Perhaps you can attend with us. I'm sure you would like to see more of this place than the inside of an orphanage."

"Splendid idea!" Marie said, clasping her hands. "I was planning to take Rose along with me. She doesn't have enough fun. You should come, sir!"

"Which play is it?" asked Peter.

"Twelfth Night," Marie replied. "It's organized by Mrs. Swanney—she used to live here, you know, and lets us attend the functions for free."

"Would that extend to me?" Peter asked. "I'm a stranger to her."

"Don't worry. I'll do the talking. Would you like to come?"

"Yes, I think I would." Despite his mixed emotions, he was fascinated by the idea of venturing into town—seeing more of the Mer and how they lived.

Rose stared at him from behind her glass of water. Though she kept her face straight, there was approval in her expression.

He was baffled, then, when she retreated to the kitchen after dinner. Hearing the sound of dishes being cleaned, he wondered how long she planned to hide.

He stood at the window, taking deep breaths. Would Rose allow him to help with the washing? A conversation remained unfinished; he could not go to sleep without patching up whatever had been disturbed.

"Psst!"

186

Peter jumped. He had not noticed Marie behind him.

She waited with clasped hands, something knowing in her smile. Had she guessed what happened in the yard earlier?

"You're taking too long," she whispered, folding the tablecloth. "She's washing dishes because she let Cook out early. I'm sure you're more important than dishes."

A clatter of silverware punctuated her words.

"She's washing slowly, too." Marie hugged the tablecloth and stepped back. "If you don't become more talkative than dishes, you'll be here longer than necessary." She dipped into a curtsy. "Good night, My Lord. I shall keep everyone distracted."

Peter listened to her footsteps fade up the stairs. Marie was right; surely he could be more talkative than silverware.

In silence he approached the kitchen door. Rose was trying to lift some dishes onto a shelf too high for her. He did not have a conversation starter, but could at least be helpful.

Pushing the door in, he said, "Allow me."

Rose set them down, sighing. She was quiet for so long that he wondered if she was ignoring him. At last she stepped back and reached for a cloth.

"It's not a problem if my hands aren't wet," she mumbled.

"Or you could ask for help." Peter lifted the dishes before Rose had time to change her mind. "There is no shame in it."

She watched him place the dishes on the problematic shelf. Peter wondered at the hurt her silence brought him.

Rose's stubbornness tried at his patience. Peter wished she would look him in the eye; there was one way to achieve that. He decided not to mince words, addressing the matter at heart.

"You said you weren't going to hide in the kitchen. You promised."

She stared at the cloth in her hands. Peter waited, preparing to be pushed away—preparing to learn she had changed her mind since they last spoke.

"I was trying to save you, Peter," she said under her breath. "I can't seem to do anything right around you."

"Save me? I don't recall you doing anything wrong."

"You don't need another woman to make you marry her," Rose said, taking a step back. "It was inconsiderate."

Peter was torn between amusement and rejection. "I don't recall you doing anything wrong," he said. "I remember a beautiful woman telling me that she loved me. I don't think she knew how desperately I needed to hear it."

Rose listened, a storm in her eyes.

"I understand things can be said on the spur of a moment," he added reluctantly. "If you didn't mean those words, I suppose you could take them back. You're allowed to." *I hope you won't.*

She stared at her feet for what seemed like an eternity. Peter waited, bracing himself for the worst, knowing he could not drag her down the path he wanted against her will.

If Rose should admit that she had spoken without thinking, he would carry on as if it did not shatter him. He would pretend she had not given him hope for the first time in years.

"I won't take them back," Rose said. Her voice was soft, the words powerful. "I meant what I said. Perhaps I could have phrased things better. I shall have to be unladylike again."

"It's not unladylike to be yourself!" he cried. "I want to

hear what *you* feel, Rose, not what you think is expected of you."

"Very well." Rose tossed the cloth aside.

Peter knew that what was coming would direct their future in a definite way. If he said the wrong thing, she would never bare her heart to him again.

She began: "This town has become my home, Peter, despite its imperfections. I know my neighbors. I learned how to haggle in the marketplace. The girls in this house cared for me before they knew what I was."

"I'm glad," Peter said. "I'm glad you found a home here. It means you weren't alone."

"Well." Rose turned to the window, wringing her hands. "This is what I have been trying to say but not phrasing correctly. My life is here—and there is little for me on the *other side*. Nothing changed for years and years, until you appeared. I fell in love with *you*, not the thought of a new life, or returning to the country, or having luxuries."

She waited, staring into the night. Waiting, he knew, for reassurance that she was not making a fool of herself.

Peter braced himself. His response would decide how the conversation ended. She had done enough talking of her own; it was his turn to risk being hurt.

"So did I," Peter said. "I fell in love with *you*. I'm not trying to be a hero, staying like I am. I want to be with you. If you asked me to live here, I would. This is not my home, but neither would *that place* be if I was forced to walk away."

"You will understand, then," said Rose, her tone steadier than it had been moments before. "The only circumstance in which I might be compelled to leave would be to marry you. It isn't that I want the status. I don't care about the money. I *will not* return to that place as a poor soul you rescued from scandal."

"I wish you would be unladylike more often," he admitted, after a pause. "I've had enough of guessing-games for the rest of my life."

Rose let out a nervous laugh. "I suppose it would make some things simpler."

"Could we stop thinking of this place as a home for poor souls?" he asked. "It is the home of the woman I love, and I want to marry her. Could we talk then?"

Peter watched Rose straighten her shoulders. On her expression there was a glow. At last he had said the right thing.

Rose stepped forward, closing the space between them. "Yes, we can talk," she said. "Have a seat. I'll fix tea."

"No," he said. "I want to help."

"All right—you can clear the table. There are dishes I haven't gotten to yet."

Peter did as he was told, glad for something to do. Work would serve as a distraction to his nerves as he braced himself for an important conversation.

The air might have been cleared, but emotions remained to grapple with.

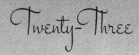

Twenty-Three

STOP BEING LADYLIKE, ROSE THOUGHT. SHE ARRANGED TEA things on the table, placing them in order, seeking the distraction of routine. *Stop being perfect.*

Love leaves no room for perfection.

She contemplated Peter's comment about being herself, rather than clinging to behaviors she taught her own pupils. It made her question the motions that had been her strength since Mother died.

How much discomfort might have been avoided if she had not hidden behind a mask? Where had she gotten the idea that every gentleman should be kept guessing? When was it decided that they deserved such treatment?

Rose wondered about the boundaries drawn by expectation. When did she stop being *ladylike*, choosing instead to be stubborn? Peter left a hurtful engagement for his own sanity, a choice many would criticize. At what point did a man stop being *masculine* and cross the line into cowardice?

She did not know what cowardice meant anymore. Peter

was many things, but she could not call him a coward. His courage was quiet but real.

Peter drew her chair at the table. Rose smiled at him and took her seat. Buying time, she poured water into the cups.

Nothing made sense, but she could not return to the *propriety* that had been a barrier. It no longer fit their narrative.

"You never told me what your fear is," Rose said, returning to their conversation in the garden. "If not marriage, what is it?"

Peter did not flinch at her question. He must have come to a similar conclusion: Honesty was the only way to move forward.

How she wished to move forward, to hold his gaze and see his soul. Only the table remained to stop her from doing something bolder than saying she loved him.

"Signing a contract is easy." Peter stared into his cup, as though hoping words would materialize in the liquid. "You marry a person in front of people whose opinions matter. It's what a lot of people do, you know, where I'm from. I must have taught myself to think of it that way in order to stomach it."

"I suppose that's a way to cope," she said, "but unhappiness follows, if it isn't something you want."

"No, dear." Rose's heart leaped at the word *dear;* Peter did not appear to notice, focused on the words in his head. "I was already unhappy. Grief made my mother temperamental; I could no longer recognize her. Sybil also noticed a change, but the pressure on her is not so great. I wasn't finished grieving when all of a sudden the only thing I could do right was make a favorable match."

His voice became thick with bitterness.

"Mother wants to keep our old friends. Appearance was always important to her, more so than she would admit. When Father died, she became paranoid of losing our connections. You see, he possessed a charisma I don't. Compared to him, I'm friendless." He paused. "Come to think of it, I had friends before I was engaged. I'm not sure what happened to them."

"Did they leave?"

Peter reached for the sugar; she noticed that his hand trembled. "Their visits became sporadic. A few attended that joke of a ball, but only to put their names in the guest list. It could be that they noticed something strange in me, and no longer wanted awkward conversations."

"They saw you hurting and did nothing," she said, angry.

"What can you do when a person stops listening? I'm not without blame. They stopped writing and so did I. My uncle was always ready to offer advice, yet I never asked. The only thing that mattered was not disappointing my mother."

He stirred the tea, stirred, stirred...

"All I had to do was marry Lady Meredith. Signing that paper would end the rants, so I could return to my library and finish grieving. My reward for doing something right." His smile was ironic. "Instead, I disappeared. Who knows what rumors are spinning about where I went?"

"I'm sure they're nothing like the truth," Rose offered. "No one will guess that you wound up by the coast where Merpeople live, playing music for starry-eyed orphans."

Her reward was a smile that broke through his pained expression. "Yes, and I would not change anything, Rose. Believe me."

"I believe you." She wanted to reassure him that she was

no longer trying to *save him.* She trusted that, after all he'd been through, he knew his emotions.

Something of his demeanor was different. The fairy-tale prince was no longer invincible; his humanity added to the beauty. Instances before, she had been vulnerable in front of him. Now he had dropped his guard, trusting her enough to show her his hurt.

"I'm afraid of disappointing people," Peter said, answering her question. "Already you have noticed I am not very expressive. I'm not romantic with words. I don't know how to flirt, having never practiced. After all, only a signature was required of me."

"You're blind." *So very blind.* "Everything you've done has been romantic. Sitting in the kitchen for days, listening to girls do needlework. I no longer believe you were only here to hide from your mother."

"I'm glad you understood that," said Peter after an embarrassed pause. "Though I'll still argue that I'm not romantic."

"We'll agree to disagree."

Peter had forgotten about the teacup, watching her with such fixation that she began to wonder if he could see her fluttering heart. The young man who claimed not to be romantic managed to get past her defenses with his constant, reassuring presence.

He hesitated before taking her hand. She did not pull away; the tug-of-war was over, Rose cheerfully defeated. The air filled with a strange enchantment which made the colors around her brighter. Her breath became shallow; she ignored her tea and stared at him. Let the drink go cold.

It was impossible, on later reflection, to figure out who began the kiss. Who stood up first? Where had fear and caution gone? The enchantment swept her away. By the time she tumbled back to earth, they were holding one another as if life depended on it. Rose was astonished by how perfectly she fit in his arms.

She could not allow him to return home alone. She would not release him into the world where someone else might catch him. He was her past, he was her future, but most importantly, he was her present.

She would never again find happiness in the mundane. If she sent him away on that horse, he would tear out her heart and take it with him.

No, he was her present.

Uncontrolled as the ocean breeze, words slipped from her mouth. They came from her tired soul after days of ladylike stubbornness. "I will go with you."

Peter's breath caught, but he did not respond with a question. She allowed him to enjoy his victory; she, also, was unable to say another word.

The man claimed not to be romantic. Of course he could not see his actions, how they spoke of love. He did not know that his gaze was captivating as the sea on a summer day. He did not know how he glowed when happy.

Inside of his shell lurked a natural longing to help others. It was warm like the sun when he was comfortable to use it; even his silence thawed ice. Before he was dropped in this place by a horse, he had stifled that wish in order to please others.

There had been no one to save him from a cruel voice telling him he was not good enough. No wonder he had been thirsty to have someone love him and *say* that they did. Rose refused to think that doing so made her *unladylike,* for now the sun shone on her, deliciously warm.

Tired and excited, comfortable yet blushing, they followed an unspoken agreement. Nothing would be lost if they waited a bit to leave. The outside world would be cruel to both of them when they returned.

Rose focused for the moment on how deeply she had fallen.

Twenty-Four

MEREDITH COULD NOT MOVE. PAIN HAD WOKEN HER, BUT SHE could not discern its origin. It was stronger than the grief she experienced after Mother's death. It rivaled the helplessness that she knew when her freedom was stolen. It was ruthless as the guilt that bound her after she shoved Peter.

Her memory worked through fog as she revisited the moments before she lost consciousness.

Grumbacher's speech put things into perspective. He wanted to kill the Mermaid, the heritage she had been ashamed of. Now this part of her became dear: *She did not want the Mermaid to die.*

Meredith spent her life angry that ocean-blood set her apart from other ladies. It was the reason Lord Bannister treated her like something foul, robbing her of the option to fall in love.

Something in her died slowly. It floundered in the fibers of her being, gasped for air, no—gasped for *sea salt.*

Meredith forced her eyes to open. *Sea salt.* It had been

too long since she had the water she needed. She would ask for it, if she could find her voice. She would tell Grumbacher that it was a misunderstanding and she did not *want* to kill the Mermaid.

He said that the matter was never meant to be a secret, yet Lord Bannister kept it from her. She would plead her case; it had not been fair, it had been against their agreement, and she did not hate herself enough to die.

Meredith lay on a bed in an unfamiliar room. Someone changed her into a nightgown—she chose not to dwell too much on *who;* it was the least of her concerns. She was sprawled on the bed like a rag doll.

It seemed too comfortable a bed for a prisoner. Even the window was open, curtains fluttering as a breeze slipped in.

She was not tied up—it would be a wasted effort, she knew, for she could not move.

The East Wing, she realized in a panic. In her mind flashed the memory of the dark corridor where she sensed someone watching her. *I am in the East Wing.*

Meredith lifted her head a half inch before it became taxing. Her breath came in gasps, beads of sweat on her face.

With a sinking feeling, she understood that it was too late. Even if she should manage to speak, her voice had never mattered; that would not change now.

The madman intended to kill the Mermaid, and there was nothing she could do about it. The reason for her pain was horrifically simple: Part of her flailed and fought to remain. It had a voice but could not scream. The only sound she could produce was a frightened whimper.

She did not sleep, forcing herself to remain present

while the part of her died. Tears mixed with her sweat. The part of her existence she had scorned now slipped from her.

If someone had deigned to ask whether she *wanted* to be 'rid of the curse,' would she have accepted? Had she disliked it so much that she would consent to its slaughter?

No. No. Never had she hated herself so much that she wanted to die. The least she could do was be present as the Mermaid slipped away.

Voices reached her from the door. Not willing to be found awake, she forced her breath to steady and pretended to be unconscious. It was not difficult when movement and speech were impossible.

An unfamiliar voice spoke: "Agnes says she didn't wake when she changed her. The girl is out cold."

Grumbacher responded. "Perhaps it is better that way. The process will be free of pain. It might be over before she wakes."

Say something, she pleaded with herself. *He might listen.*

"What of Mr. Greer?" asked the stranger. "Should we be worried that he will interfere again?"

"That oaf of a groundskeeper won't be a problem."

"He broke the door down. I hope he's been taken care of."

"He's locked up."

Gideon, Meredith thought with a start. She remembered his note about wanting to protect her. Had he known about this?

Grumbacher broke into her thoughts: "She isn't asleep. Pity. Good evening, Lady Meredith."

Anger gave her the energy to open her eyes —brokenness and helplessness combined to create a storm. Though she could not use anger to crawl off of the bed, she was certain he could see it.

The smile vanished from Grumbacher's countenance.

Behind him lurked a tall, pallid man. His face was emotionless as he watched Meredith through spectacles perched on the bridge of his nose.

Meredith recognized the prickling sensation from earlier. She was certain that this man had been watching from the shadows when she crept into the East Wing. Had he been in the mansion this entire time?

"I was hoping you wouldn't wake up," Grumbacher told her. His assistant remained silent behind him. "I'll call for that mute maid of yours to bring food."

Eat, pleaded the part of her that knew it was dying. Sustenance would help it in this battle. Perhaps it would survive—she would be able to find forgiveness for herself.

Anger spurred her pride, though. Agnes was no friend of hers if she had known about this and not tried to help.

Gideon, wherever he had been locked up, was the only real friend she ever had.

Meredith would not eat the food they gave her. Grumbacher was no fool; he knew salt water would help her, and was not foolish enough to give her a weapon.

If the rest of her died, there would be no guilt. There was nothing left for her in this world.

"I know it might appear a heavy burden," Grumbacher said, seeing her defiance. "No doubt you are in pain and confused. We have done what we could to make you comfortable."

How dare he? A soft bed and an open window—they were things she did not notice in this haze. The sweat that bathed her and the voice inside of her begging for mercy, those were the only things of which she was aware.

"I see that negotiating with you will be futile," he added, crossing the room to a table in the corner. Opening a drawer, he sorted through its contents. "You have enough fire in you to get through this treatment. Already, you outlived the part that killed your mother."

Why did he keep implying that Mother died of a treatment? She was poisoned! Meredith had been the one to find her dead in the dining room.

Unless there was a thicker story behind it. Unless Lord Bannister fabricated a lie out of something darker, truths he would never deign to tell her.

"Very well," said Grumbacher. "You refuse to eat. I will delay the second part of the treatment for a few hours. It's clear you need time to think things through." Glancing at his assistant, he added, "Or be persuaded."

"Perhaps," said the assistant, not looking at Meredith as he spoke of her, "she would be persuaded by knowing *what* the second part of the treatment is."

Reluctance crossed Grumbacher's face. "She is a child, Appleby. It's not her fault. She was not told about any of this."

"She is not unintelligent," said the other. "Ignorance is no mercy. Lady Meredith, the second part of the treatment involves an injection. It will be the end of you if you haven't eaten. We will return in the morning to see if you have changed your mind."

Appleby slipped back into the corridor. Grumbacher lingered for a tense moment.

When he looked at Meredith, she might have believed that

his remorse was genuine. His slumped shoulders betrayed a flicker of humanity. "I have a daughter," he whispered. "I mean you no harm. I hope that, in the morning, you will eat."

Feet dragging, he slipped into the corridor after his assistant, leaving Meredith in horror of what Appleby had told her.

A part of her continued to die, while the rest refused to give in.

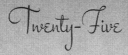

Twenty-Five

THE NEXT MORNING, PETER WAITED IN MRS. WHITTLE'S parlor while everyone slept. He had determined to speak to her first thing. He refused to think too much about it, fearing he would lose his nerve.

The kiss had given him certainty, that most intimate brush with Rose's gentle soul. Her tender embrace had answered all of his questions. It was now clear to him that they both knew what they wanted.

Rose had made her wishes known; it was his turn.

He waited for Mrs. Whittle, knowing that she was an early riser. Unable to sit still, he examined some drawings on the back wall. They were portraits of young women he assumed to be former pupils.

Peter examined the sketch of a pale girl with sad eyes. Fondness stirred in his heart; he knew well who it was. Even when sketched as a child, Rose was very much herself. She sat primly on a wooden chair, hands clasped on her lap. Familiar sadness lingered in young Rose's eyes. How recently had her mother died when the likeness had been captured? Grief clung to her like the soft material of her dress.

Peter exhaled, finding that he shared her pain. Rose had been forced to grow up so early that her smile was rare. She became a teacher to girls who were not much older than herself. Even when he did at last whisk her out of this place, she would always see the world with that motherly instinct.

There came footsteps behind him as Mrs. Whittle entered the room. "You're a proper owl, sir," she said, closing the door. "The sun has scarcely risen."

Peter wondered at the knowing way in which she smiled. Perhaps she knew what he was going to say. There was not much that got past Mrs. Whittle.

She motioned to an armchair. "Have a seat, My Lord. Something troubles you."

Though restless, he obliged, taking the indicated seat. She went to her writing-desk and opened it, giving him seconds to get his speech together.

"I wouldn't say it's a trouble, Mrs. Whittle." Looking at her, he stated the reason for his presence. "I want to marry Lady Rose, and I have come to ask for your consent."

It was the second time Peter asked for a woman's hand, the first time he asked it in love. When he posed this question to Lord Bannister, there was no emotion involved. It had been a business choice to please others. The question was more frightening this time, for the response could, in truth, hurt him.

A spark of emotion lit Mrs. Whittle's face, but her smile held when she spoke. "I wondered why it was taking so long. It's a shame that her father isn't here. He would want to see her loved and happy."

Peter waded through his memory for an image of Lord

Julian Finch. He had been a boy the last time he saw Lord Julian alive.

Lord Finch had been a confident man with a great thirst for change. He had the rare quality of believing people were good at heart. It was this quality that possibly led to his death by poison later.

Would it have been frightening to ask Lord Julian for Rose's hand? He remembered Lord Finch as a kind man, but would that kindness extend to someone vying for his daughter's heart?

"I know he would have liked you," Mrs. Whittle said. "Countless Arabella told me much about him. Your families were close, I believe."

"Yes," he said. "He was friends with my father."

Mrs. Whittle nodded. "Well," she said, addressing his request with the dignity of a parent, "as the honor has fallen on me, Lord Everly, you have my permission—so long as this is what you both want."

Peter hoped that his frustration was not evident. Everybody seemed to think that, because he had been unhappy with one engagement, he would never be able to commit to another.

"I *want* to marry her, Mrs. Whittle," he said with feeling. "Lady Rose has also made her wish clear."

"That *is* a bit of a surprise," said Mrs. Whittle. "It gives me relief."

She went to the window, pushing the curtains aside to let light into the room. Peter blinked, wondering how the sun had come up so quickly.

"Rose never says what she wants," the woman continued. "Until now, she seemed to think she did not have the right to plan a happy life. She never asked for more than she was given. That's why I worried and asked for your help."

Her words served to give him confidence. No one knew Rose better than her second mother. If Mrs. Whittle had noticed a positive change, he could not be doing the wrong thing.

"Then again," Mrs. Whittle added, beaming, "you *have* been here for quite a while. Patience wins most battles, sir. You shall make her happy, and I am grateful that your presence convinced her that she is worth more than this."

"Thank you," he said, as the nerves abated a little. "Though you must know, Rose does not think she is leaving a bad life. She is grateful to you, Mrs. Whittle. I am certain she won't forget this place." Pausing, he added, "Neither will I. After I've settled some personal matters, I plan on returning. I intend to patron this orphanage and, if possible, establish it someplace else."

The woman smiled her approval. "I understand how you managed to change her mind. You've got a good heart, and I knew it from the start. I can smell a bad egg from miles away, sir. Your honesty was refreshing. I would not have entrusted my eldest daughter to a man I didn't like."

Peter said nothing, moved by her words. He glanced at the carpet and wondered if the tasks he had taken up were beyond his ability.

If Rose sent him home alone, things would be different. Peter might not have been able to do more than manage the business. He would rot away in his library, looking at ledgers. All the while, he would be wishing to return to this orphanage, where he left his heart in the hands of a stubborn woman who underestimated her fire.

Rose's fire would give him the encouragement he needed.

"Well," said Mrs. Whittle. "I suppose you are lingering because you need advice."

"Yes." He cleared his throat, preparing to address the second matter of his day. "Now I have to ask her properly. I'd rather it not be here, but I don't know where to go. Believe it or not, during my stay, I have learned very little about my surroundings."

"It would have been unsafe to take you into town," Mrs. Whittle said. "Strangers are noticed in these parts. Your intentions are not yet known to others, and I doubt you would be received kindly."

"What about the parish play?" he asked, feeling a stab of disappointment. The thought of seeing other people had excited him, but if Mrs. Whittle thought it dangerous...

"The parish is around the corner, and this event was arranged by people connected to me. There will not be many strangers. Besides, I assume you will not stay much longer than that. After you've asked the question, it won't be so easy to wait."

Peter wondered why her words brought color to his cheeks. "Well," he said, trying to steer the conversation back, "next time I come, I would like to see the places that need help."

"You will have a proper tour next time, sir. You'll return as the husband of one of our own. I assure you, it will win many friends." Mrs. Whittle retook her seat, addressing his question. "You could go to the beach. Return to the place where Rose took you that first day; it's safe when the sun is up. A picnic is as good a place as any for a proposal."

The cliff, he thought, baffled that he hadn't thought of it before.

There *was* a place he knew of that was private, a place with the benefit of being meaningful to Rose. That cliff was the setting for her loneliest memories, but Peter was convinced that he could give it one happy memory. If all went well, it would put an end to the sad chapters of her life.

"Thank you," he said, unnerved by the task at hand.

"I'll prepare a basket for you," said Mrs. Whittle. "Convince Rose to join you before she decides it's a day for work. She ought to be up soon; she rarely sleeps in."

"Can I help?" Peter could not bear another half hour in this room, anticipating the most important question of his life.

"If you like," said Mrs. Whittle. "Help me make sandwiches. It might settle your nerves."

Peter smiled. She already knew that he was nervous; there was no point denying it.

Rose had been right: The forsaken Mer district had been the place where he learned to make his own decisions.

Twenty-Six

ROSE WOKE TO A PREMONITION THAT GREAT CHANGE WAS coming. Already, her life was radically different from the routine she had built after Mother's death.

While nursing the strange young man to health, she never imagined he would take her heart. Even when she recognized Peter, she expected him to leave as soon as he was able. Instead, he stayed for days and days, waiting for her to answer a question. In his quiet manner, he dispelled her darkest memories.

Rose sat at the edge of her bed, staring in wonder out the window.

The night before, he had claimed a kiss.

If Mother were alive, she would be ecstatic. She had been a hopeless romantic, speaking wistfully of the day Rose would find love. How delighted she would be to know it was Peter clamoring for her daughter's heart, rather than a stranger!

He loves me, Mother, Rose thought. *I don't understand how.*

"Well?" Marie's voice startled her. "How was it?"

"How was what?"

She sensed, rather than saw, Marie rolling her eyes. "The kiss."

Glad for the darkness that hid her red cheeks, Rose wondered if it was worth denying that there had been a kiss. Her joy was so great that she wanted to share it with *someone*. Mother might not have been alive, but it did not mean she was alone. In the past, she had trusted Marie with the secret of her identity. Why should a kiss be any different?

"How do you know?" Rose asked.

"I saw him standing at the window after dinner. It was obvious that he wanted to see you. I've read enough novels to know where that leads."

Rose clasped her hands, wrestling with joy and self-consciousness. Love had caused her to toss aside regular behaviors. If Marie noticed a romance unfolding, had the other girls done the same?

"Well?" Marie asked. "How was it?"

Needing to move, Rose went to the wardrobe, tossing words over her shoulder. "It…it was…"

How to describe the sensation of being kissed? *How* to describe the thrill of knowing someone had fallen for her? She never thought it could happen, having gone out of her way to be uninteresting.

Rose always feared that a man who fell for her might learn her secrets by seeing her eyes. Her efforts were successful, until the day a man appeared who *was* in her past, who formed a part of her secret. Peter had proved himself to be the one person she couldn't fool.

"It was freeing," Rose said, settling on the emotion she

experienced in his arms. There was such lightness when love set her free from falsehoods.

"You deserve it," said Marie. "You've given up enough to help others. I always suspected love would find you."

"You'll find love, too." It was impossible not to feel guilt; Marie dreamed of her own happy ending. "Surely it finds those who seek it."

Rose hesitated at the contents of her wardrobe. Instinct made her wish to dress well. The drab blue dresses she had used for years did no justice to her new world of color.

Instinct had done good things thus far. She decided to trust it, choosing a floral frock that she saved for holidays.

Marie did not comment on Rose's selection. "When looking for love, you become choosy."

"That isn't a bad thing," Rose said, closing the wardrobe before she could have second thoughts. "You've got to be careful when picking the person to share your life with."

"Is that what you've done?" Marie asked. "Have you chosen to share your life with him?"

Rose did not know how to reply. "I…"

Marie sat up, beaming. "Let me do your hair," she said, not asking questions. "You're terrible at it."

Half an hour later, Rose descended the stairs, grappling with her inner voice. It told her she ought to have chosen a plain frock. It told her that she looked ridiculous with a flower clip in her hair. It made her long for the plainness she used as a shield.

Peter appeared at the foot of the stairs. "Good morning," he said, offering a hand to help her down.

"Hello," Rose said, accepting his aid. The touch gave her a thrill. "This is where we parted. Did you sleep at all?"

"I'm an early riser," he said, stuttering a little. "Would you like to have a picnic? Breakfast outside, I mean."

Hours before, Rose might have found an excuse to slip away. Lesson plans, gardening, or a feigned illness. She no longer had the will to resume their tug-of-war.

"Yes, that sounds lovely," she replied. "I'll tell Mrs. Whittle—"

"She already knows."

Something in his demeanor changed; Rose glimpsed a touch of anxiety. Had he doubted that she would accept his offer to picnic? Perhaps; she had given him reason to think she would hide.

Rose followed him into the kitchen, where a picnic basket waited for them.

Choosing not to ask questions, she followed him to the garden—but he did not stop there, leading her through the gate to the road. Then, he ventured to the spot where her cliff was located, finding the entrance without effort.

"You remembered how to find it," she said, pleased.

"I don't often forget secret passageways," he said. "Er— ladies first, I suppose."

Rose smiled at his reluctance to follow etiquette. "I know this place," she said, slipping down to the precipice that had been her refuge. "You're more likely to fall than I."

"I suppose you're right," Peter said, stepping in after her. "I do have a tendency to fall. I've tumbled down a flight of stairs, then off of a horse…"

It was the first time she heard him jest about the events that brought him to her door. He must have begun to heal from those wounds if he could speak of them so lightly.

Peter stepped in front of her before finishing his sentence: "And I've fallen in love. That counts, too."

His words, unprompted and raw, gave her a surge of joy. She had wasted so much time worrying that her sentiments would not be returned, or that they would be a trap for him.

"I hope that fall wasn't painful," Rose said.

"It was, a bit," he said, placing the basket on the ground. "But I'm grateful. If I had not felt myself crash into love, it would mean I was dead inside. Because of you, I can be sure that I'm not."

Rose wondered why he had chosen this spot, all the while holding a suspicion in her heart. He did not often express himself with words, relying instead on actions. If he was using words, forming his thoughts in front of her, this must be more than a picnic.

Rose's suspicions did not lessen her astonishment when he knelt before her.

"I don't have a ring," he began. "Not yet…"

Seven days earlier, Rose might have fled before he could continue. Instead, she stood and waited. She had done enough talking about the future she wanted with him. How badly she wished to hear that he wanted it, too!

"Please," he continued, "for a few minutes, forget *what* you are—and forget *what* I am—because all I have ever seen is who you are."

Rose nodded, pushing from her mind *words* that had served as barriers since they found each other. There were no titles, no scandals; *wealth* was not a mark on him, *orphan* did not define her. She forgot these things, focusing on who he was: A brave heart, an open mind, someone who had been hurt once and now exposed himself once more.

Peter asked the question she never thought she would hear. "Rose, will you marry me?"

She basked in the fairy tale her life had become. This

was a happy ending and a beginning full of promise. Even as he gave her the power to hurt him, she resolved never to do so.

Rose touched his cheek, bending down so they were level. One word would suffice to put away their awkward beginning and start anew. She was no longer afraid to follow him into the unknown.

"Yes."

The word floated for several heartbeats. Peter stared at her; his features spoke of bafflement. He must be fearing a long-winded speech, or perhaps for her to change her mind. She needed him to know that she was being herself, not *being ladylike.*

From that moment on, she would never be anything but herself.

"Yes." Rose said the word again in a whisper.

The whisper must have been louder than a shout. His shock gave way to joy, and a tear slid down his face when the truth set in.

At the end of the world, he found that elusive joy he thought was stolen from him. She let him pull her to his heart, and marveled that the same could be said for her. At the end of the world, she had waited; it was there that love found her.

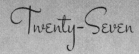

Twenty-Seven

MEREDITH COULD NOT OPEN HER EYES.

Are you there? she asked the dying part of her—the Mermaid. *Have they killed you?*

Am I alone?

MEREDITH KNEW she was in a dream. She stood on the landing of the stairs at the Bannister home. Voices drifted from above. Guests had gathered, waiting for Lord Bannister to finish speaking.

They were expecting a speech from Peter.

Dream-Meredith knew she needed to return to the party. She could not risk embarrassing Lord Bannister by being late.

She turned and froze. Peter stood behind her.

Not Peter, said a tiny voice, a splinter of awareness. *I am asleep.*

The fact of being asleep did not make his expression less

frightening. His blue eyes were cold, as if carved from stone. She would not be able to get up the stairs without touching him, the last thing she wanted to do.

Meredith had never seen Peter angry. She knew he was often frustrated because of her; even in those instances, the young man was never willing to fight. The dream version of him wore a clouded expression, giving no clue about what he was thinking.

She had seen those eyes in the mirror. He had stolen her mask; now he wore it.

"We need to go up," dream-Meredith said to Peter. She spoke in a meek voice, knowing how easily he could shove her down the stairs. She did not wish to make him lose his temper.

"You know how this ends," said Peter. "One of us will fall."

Her skin crawled. She struggled to follow the narrative as it unfolded in her head. Her body was playing a cruel trick, trapping her in sleep, reminding her that one always did pay for their sins in life.

"I'm sorry," dream-Meredith pleaded. "I should have told you why I needed help."

"Yes," said Peter, not moving. "Everything is your fault."

She heard the cling of a spoon on glass—Lord Bannister changing the subject, announcing that a speech would be made. "We're going to be late," she said. "Let me through."

"I don't take orders from you anymore," he said.

Meredith wondered why she had never noticed how tall he was. "Please," she said. "I can explain."

"What ever for? You won't get forgiveness," he said. "I don't care why you needed me. Do you not yet understand, Mermaid? No one loves you."

I am the one speaking, said the voice of reason, even as she cringed from the sound of truth. "I know."

"Put an end to everything," said Peter. "Who will grieve?"

Meredith might have been in agony for most of her life, but she never wanted to stop living. The double of Peter standing before her had no mercy or compassion. He would not understand her reasons, even if she begged.

"No," she said. "I don't want to die."

"No one loves you," he repeated.

She nodded, swallowing. "I still don't want to die."

"You make everyone unhappy," he said. "Do you think that will change?"

"It won't," Meredith said. "I don't need to be dead."

"Mermaid, you pollute the planet by breathing its air."

"This is a dream." At last she took control of her own actions. "You aren't Peter. He would never say those things, even if he thought them."

"You're right," said the impostor. "If not him, who am I?"

She had no time to reply, for he had shoved her into the abyss of a nightmare. The falling seemed never to end as she plummeted into reality.

MEREDITH DID NOT REALIZE at first that she was the one who screamed. Her voice had woken her. It was inhuman, the cry of a creature not worthy to live. Fear gave her the energy she needed to sob; misery gave her what she needed to be miserable.

"I'm sorry," she pleaded—for the air to hear, for the silence to absorb, wanting to rip the words from her chest. "I never meant to hurt you."

A hand rested on her shoulder. Opening her eyes, she saw Agnes peering down at her.

To her astonishment, the mute maid whispered. Her voice was a rasp, only audible if Meredith held her breath.

"You...m—muss—st eat..."

"Go," whispered Meredith, more frightened of the maid than she had been of Peter's phantom. "You're no friend."

"But—but—Lady Me—Meredith—"

"Concealing the truth is no better than lying. Leave me."

Agnes exhaled. She turned and left the room; Meredith stared at the door until her footsteps faded.

Her eyelids became heavy again. *Have you died?* she asked the Mermaid.

Meredith felt the silence, rather than hear it. Something that had been a part of her was gone.

Voices reached through her fog. Meredith heard sentences but could only make out words: *Won't fool her— Will* die!*—No one else can talk to her...*

A crash caused the bed to tremble. Her eyes snapped open. Gideon knelt beside her, gasping. He had been shoved; she noted an angry purple bruise over his left eye.

"What have you done to her?" he whispered. "She's pale. She…"

"If she does not eat, she'll be dead," said Grumbacher behind him. "She sent the maid away. I have reason to suspect you might be more convincing."

Gideon reached for her hand. "I was late," he whispered to her. "Meredith, I was late. I'm sorry. You need to eat."

Grumbacher continued: "If you can *behave*, I'll allow you to stay. When it is over, leave with her."

"I will not hold her down while you stick a needle in

her," Gideon hissed, not releasing her hand. "You have no soul, Grumbacher."

"Perhaps not," the man shot back, "but the plan was not for her to die. That injection ensures that the *rest* of her will not succumb. Talk sense into her."

He left with a slam of the door.

Gideon closed his eyes, wincing at the sound. His grip on her hand tightened regardless of physical pain. She watched him catch a breath before saying, "Meredith, I know my word is nothing to what you've been through. You need to eat."

She shook her head. *Easier to follow the Mermaid. I tried to kill a man.* All of these things crossed her mind, but the words that slipped through her mouth were simple and so very broken.

"No one loves me."

She wondered at the relief that crept through her after the words escaped. No one loved her, no one ever had, and the world would be better without her. People would no longer use her; there would be no more rejection.

Gideon shook his head. "That isn't true."

"No one does!"

"I do," he said, slowly. "I don't pretend to know you well, but I do love you. Let me know you better! Don't leave me in this ugly world."

She was puzzled. Instances before, Peter in her dream had told her to vanish. Gideon's words were the opposite, his sentiment making her speechless. He was little more than a stranger, he knew nothing of her. He wanted her to stay.

How *desperately* she wished to say yes. Perhaps he saw that desire in her eyes, for he continued, emboldened.

"There's broth for you," he whispered. "Give me a chance. I'll show you that life is worth living."

Meredith was drawn to his kindness; it gave her strength, it was addictive, she wished for more. She tried propping herself on her elbows with little success. He caught her, letting her lean on his arm.

Gideon's green eyes were like forests. How had she not noticed?

"Bannister killed her," whispered Meredith, an epiphany descending on her despite her frailty. "He killed my mother. Now Grumbacher has killed the Mermaid who lived in me. She is dead!"

He did not answer about Bannister, instead responding to her words about the Mermaid. "You're more than that. You're so much more."

"Do you believe him?" she asked, thinking of what Grumbacher said—that if she survived, they could leave. Perhaps what remained of her would have a life, piteous as it might be.

"He does not mean for you to die. It would defeat his purpose."

Meredith wished she could heal the bruise on his eye. She could not erase the pain of a beating, but could she spare him grief? It might have been desperation, but she found it easy to believe that this man wanted her to stay.

"Where's the broth?" she asked.

"It's on the table behind me."

She noticed the fierce hope in his voice. It was a beautiful sound; she wished to hear it again. "If you help me sit, I'll try it."

Meredith knew a fresh round of pain awaited when she finished eating. However, she was not fighting for her own sake. How freeing it was to think of someone other than herself.

Sip by sip, she drank the broth. A thought crossed her mind for the first time in her life: *This broth is too salty.*

Her body had changed, somber proof that the Mermaid was dead.

Twenty-Eight

"CONGRATULATIONS," said MARIE. "YOU TOOK MY ADVICE!"

Peter sat at the table, staring at its polished surface. He had been revisiting the moment when Rose told him *yes*. He remembered the look on her face when she said it, how she whispered it a second time; he remembered her certainty.

"Thank you," he told Marie. "You were a great help."

Marie smiled, arranging napkins for tea. "You're welcome. I'm glad you listened to me. Where is Rose?"

"She went to speak with Mrs. Whittle."

After the proposal, Rose had gone in search of her adopted mother. It was a conversation she needed to have alone. Though Peter wondered what they were saying, his heart told him he would never know.

He was happy instead to bask in Rose's word, her *yes*.

"Maybe she's asking Mrs. Whittle how far we went to help you." Marie grinned. "If it weren't for us, she'd be hiding in the garden."

Peter laughed. Then, wanting to be helpful, he reached for a tray of silverware and put himself to work.

Marie chattered away.

"I wish I could be at the wedding. It's going to be so far from here. Seeing you two fall in love was enough, so I should count myself fortunate."

Peter stopped, heart heavy. In a better world, Rose could invite her friends to a wedding. They would make the journey and be a part of that celebration, mingling with other guests, sharing in the happy day.

However, they lived in an angry world. Merpeople could not attend weddings or shop at most places. Their presence was discouraged. Even if they managed to sneak into the celebration, the awareness remained of their being unwanted.

He glanced at Marie while she worked; there were no outward signs of her being Mer. She reminded him of Sybil, bright and cheery, seeing the best in others. Was it possible that he could bring one of Rose's friends to the wedding?

"Would you like to attend?" he asked, setting the tray aside. "You would have to be ready for a journey."

Marie looked up, speechless for the first time since he met her.

Peter continued: "Once I settle things at home, I'll send for you. I would like Rose to have one of her sisters. The question is whether you would stay after that, or prefer to return."

"Sir, I did not mean to give the task to you," she said, shoulders slumping. "It was wishful thinking. You don't have to return for me."

The idea had begun to take shape; Peter found himself unable to let go. "You could find work," he said, thinking once more of the orphanage he would build, a plan he had yet to tell Rose about. "Rose will be homesick, and it'll help to have you."

"Where would I find work? You know what I am."

"You look no different from any other lady I have met," he said. "You've had an education. Marie, there is nothing binding you here."

Marie turned away. Peter understood that she had never expected to receive an offer of this nature. It would come to her as a shock, but he thought it a good idea for many reasons.

"You don't have to answer now," he said. "I'll write when a date is set. Make your choice then."

Marie nodded, wiping an invisible crumb from the table. "Thank you," she said. "I'll give it thought."

"Please do," Peter said, and left it at that.

He hoped that she would be brave enough.

A door opened. Mrs. Whittle exited her sitting room. Behind her emerged Rose, holding an envelope. Her eyes were puffy, as if she had been crying.

"I'll help with the table," Rose said to Marie, who shook her head.

"This meal is to celebrate you two," said the redhead, smiling. "Have a seat and take a break for once in your life."

"But—"

"Sit," Marie said, pointing to the chair next to Peter.

Mrs. Whittle laughed, disappearing into the kitchen.

Peter drew the chair for Rose, who glared playfully at her sister. He smirked. Their interaction convinced him that Marie's presence at the wedding would be wonderful.

Rose took the seat, looking down at the yellowing envelope. It had been sealed with wax. She held it with reverence, as if it were sacred.

"What's that?" Peter asked.

"It's from my mother," Rose said, touching the envelope fondly. "Mrs. Whittle said she wrote it after she became sick. She asked that it be put away until the day I married. It was her way of being present at my wedding."

"You mustn't open it yet," Marie warned. "I know you'll be tempted to look."

Rose shook her head. "I'm going to respect her wishes. Maybe I won't open it. There won't be more later."

Marie watched with a sympathetic smile before joining Mrs. Whittle in the kitchen, shutting the door. Peter wondered if he had spooked her with his offer. Like Rose, she might need a bit of encouragement.

"Rose, are you all right?" he asked.

"Nostalgia," she said. "Speaking of my mother triggered memories."

He wrapped an arm around her, not caring if Marie stepped out to see. He understood her nostalgia. If he were given such a letter from his father, he would have been afraid to open it.

"You didn't tell me how much help you had from Mrs. Whittle," Rose said, eyes sparkling.

"Should I apologize?"

"No. I should, though. I never realized how stubborn I could be."

Peter shrugged. "Stubbornness isn't always a bad thing."

Rose stared at the wax seal on the envelope. "We shouldn't linger," she said, surprising him. "Mrs. Whittle thinks we're both ready to go."

"Do you feel ready?"

"I don't think I'll ever be more ready. Whether we leave

now or in a month, it will be daunting all the same. You have matters to settle."

Peter exhaled. Rose had been right to remind him of his responsibilities. He grappled with reluctance to return to his own home. It didn't matter how long he waited, there remained a mess for him to clean up. Mother would demand explanations, there would be shouting. He could not dream of a happy future until he had told the truth.

"All right," he said.

Rose touched his hand. "You are still someone's son, someone's brother. Someone's nephew. Don't you think it's time to make amends?"

Peter thought of Sybil. What had become of her after he vanished? Did Mother come to her senses after the incident, or had she shifted her controlling nature onto her daughter? The title *brother* weighed most on him; it was for Sybil that he would return. He felt urgency only to help her.

"When do we go, then?" he asked.

"Early." Rose's voice did not waver. "In the morning, so we don't waste sunlight."

The younger girls chattered as they came downstairs to join them. Peter was glad to end the subject. If he thought too much of the journey, it would be difficult to begin.

"What of the play?" he asked. "That's tomorrow."

"Marie will understand."

Peter hoped so; he did not like breaking promises.

"All right," he agreed. "We leave in the morning." It would be counterproductive to stay longer, growing accustomed to comfort and safety.

They pulled apart before the newcomers could see them.

Peter would ask Mrs. Whittle for a map. He had finished

recovering from the fall and succeeded in winning Rose's heart. Her presence gave him the courage he would need to face his family.

There was no longer any reason to delay his return.

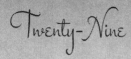

Twenty-Nine

ROSE HAD THOUGHT HER POSSESSIONS FEW. SHE DID NOT realize how much she gathered over time until faced with the task of packing it. After an hour of indecision, she settled for a change of clothes, a box of trinkets, and a comb. Mother's letter was tucked into the box.

The sun had yet to rise. Marie remained asleep, her head under a pillow. Rose decided it was best if she did not wake.

She changed into a frock suitable for travel and tied her hair with a ribbon, eschewing elaborate braids and knots for something practical.

Once finished, her gaze swept the room in which she had grown.

Rose wondered if her mother's spirit would stay in this place by the ocean. Mother chose to be with the Mer, rather than seeking out relatives. Her remains rested under the sea in a place of outcasts. Countless Arabella would have had her reasons. They were lost in the past; Rose put them out of her mind, determined to move on.

She slipped into the corridor and down the stairs,

avoiding steps that she knew creaked. A faint light glowed in the kitchen.

Peter sat at the table, poring over an old map. His belongings consisted of a battered jacket and the notebook Mrs. Whittle gave him. In it he made notes, copying parts of the map. Rose wondered if it would be a shock for him to return to a house full of riches.

"I'm sure you could take the map," she said, crossing the kitchen and reaching for the kettle. "You needn't make drawings."

"I don't want to take Mrs. Whittle's map," Peter answered. The circles under his eyes suggested he had not slept. "I've decided to go to my uncle's house first. According to this map, it's nearer."

Rose filled the kettle, feeling a prickle of unease at meeting people outside. "Do you think he would be kind to someone returning from the afterlife?" she asked, trying for morbid humor.

Peter looked up with a tired smile. "Well, you must allow him to be puzzled. He isn't unkind, though."

She prepared two cups of tea as morning stretched in streaks of orange. As of yet, she'd had no second thoughts about leaving. Perhaps, in a week, she would wake up homesick for the kitchen garden.

Rose forced these thoughts from her mind. It was important that she remain strong.

Peter did not seem to share her optimism. Seeing the stiffness of his shoulders, she asked, "What's the matter?"

He finished studying the map and folded it. "I'm wary to return. This place has been comfortable. I could have spent my days by the beach, knowing no one would look for me. I might have done that, until you reminded me of my family."

"I'm sure they are worried," Rose said. "You might think they're angry. It's possible to be angry with someone and worried for their life."

He listened, expression dark with guilt.

Rose finished gently: "The backlash will pass. You'll have a chance to tell people how you would like to be treated."

Peter stirred his tea thoughtfully. "I'm going to Uncle Theo because he has a better temperament. He is sure to be displeased, but not prone to hysterics. I hope he will listen before sending me away. I should never have stopped going to him for advice."

"You know him better than I do."

Rose allowed the subject to fade. She searched the cupboards for food that they could take on the journey.

While she folded bread and dried meat into a cloth, Peter washed both cups. He seemed to enjoy simple activities—scrubbing and drying, leaving a place better than he found it. He would not likely find opportunities to wash dishes at his estate.

When Peter finished, he sighed. There remained no reason to keep stalling. Rose put his notebook into her carpet-bag and followed him out of the kitchen.

She was startled to find Marie waiting by the door. The redhead wore her threadbare robe against the morning chill, face set with determination.

"Good morning, Rose," she said.

"I thought you were sleeping," Rose said, heart sinking. She had hoped to avoid a farewell.

Marie shook her head. "I wasn't going to come down." She twirled her untidy braid around her finger. "But—I made a decision," she said to Peter, "regarding your offer yesterday."

Rose frowned at him. "What offer?"

Marie continued: "I find it odd that you would go to the trouble of returning for me. I have spoken to Mrs. Whittle. She thought it a splendid idea, and encouraged me to accept your offer."

Some of his tension vanished. "Excellent. I'll write."

"Also," Marie said, stepping forward, "I want to remind you of something. Rose is going very far from me today. If I should learn that she is hurting, I will find you, My Lord. You won't need to return for me; I'll show up at your door with a knife. I'll do it on behalf of all the orphans making a sacrifice for her happiness. Do you understand?"

"Marie!" Rose cried.

Peter smiled at Marie, giving a slight bow. "I understand," he said. "I hope to prove myself worthy of your trust."

Marie turned a shade of red and cleared her throat. "Thank you, sir. I await your letter."

She looked at Rose, whose anger gave way to a dull ache. She didn't care what letter they were speaking of. It no longer mattered what they were planning. Their secret was shadowed by the knowledge that she would have to walk away.

"You weren't hoping to leave without saying good-bye?" Marie asked.

Rose shook her head, tears stinging her eyes. She wrapped her arms around her sister, fearing the moment might crush her.

The orphanage had been her haven and home. For most of her life, she entertained no thoughts of leaving. She learned all of its sounds and smells, knew where it leaked on rainy days, could sweep the narrow corners and climb trees.

Rose had known the ladies that came before her; she attended their weddings when they left. She watched their babies grow into children, teaching many of them to sew. She learned to find fulfillment in caring for others.

"Keep in touch," Marie said, stepping away.

"Of course. I won't forget you."

"You'll have to tell us all about the outside world—what it is like. We'll live vicariously through you."

Rose imagined Mrs. Whittle reading her letters aloud at dinner, the girls listening with rapt attention. "I promise."

Marie turned to Peter, exhaling. "You don't want to be late. I wish you both safe travels."

"You stay safe, as well," he said. "Please thank Mrs. Whittle for letting me stay. She had great patience to house a stranger who did not want to leave."

"She took a liking to you, sir. You showed interest in our corner of the world. It did not go unnoticed."

Peter took Rose's bag and said, "I found kindness. Broken souls are drawn to it like moths."

"The Moores should be finishing breakfast," Marie said. "Good luck."

She stared at Rose for a moment before hurrying upstairs. Soon they heard the sound of a bedroom door closing.

Peter kept quiet while Rose gathered herself. She appreciated not having to explain her silence. At last she opened the door and stepped out, breathing the familiar sea air. He followed her, and together they listened to a chorus of birds announcing the morning.

"Are you all right?" Peter asked, as they neared the neighbors' home.

"I am," she said. "Don't worry, Peter, I haven't changed my mind. You must understand that it feels like a dream."

They stopped at the Moores' door. Rose knocked and waited, inhaling the dewy morning air. Hearing Peter's unsteady breath, she reached for his hand.

Moments later, the door swung open. A mousey maid peered out at them, rubbing her sleepy eyes.

"Hello. I'd like to see Mr. Moore, please," Rose said, smiling. "It's about Lord Everly's horse, the one they've been caring for."

At the sound of Peter's title, the maid's eyes widened. She greeted Peter with a curtsy and said, "Yes, Miss Rose. Come inside. I'll tell Mr. Moore that you're here."

Thirty

MEREDITH BLINKED AT THE CEILING, QUESTIONS FILLING HER mind. How long had she been unconscious after the injection? Bright light poured through the window, but she had no way of knowing how long it had been since the pain stopped.

Gideon dozed on a chair nearby. The bruise on his eye had yet to vanish. Meredith wondered what motivated him to take a beating for her. Even if he thought he might love her, he knew nothing about her. Perhaps he had lied to make her eat.

Even as she thought this, logic told her otherwise. She'd been a liar for most of her life and could recognize transparency in the man before her. No one chose to get beaten if there was not some love involved. Whether he had been wise in his actions was another matter.

She remembered the Mermaid with a sinking feeling. The emptiness in her stretched on.

Meredith sat up, dread settling in the pit of her stomach.

Reaching back, she touched her shoulder, fingers brushing that spot.

Wardrobes had been designed for her with the purpose of concealing the mark of Mermaid. Most days she wished to ignore it; she might have been happy to have it vanish. However, she felt no relief when the scales came off at her touch, clinging to the sweat on her palms.

Mermaids did not have scales; the marks of Mermaid fled from her, disgusted by what she had become.

Meredith stared at her hand. Once rich and pearly, the scales were lifeless. She thought of leaves in the autumn, shattering at a touch. She did not need to look at her knee to know those scales met the same fate.

A hot tear slid down her face. No one had asked if she wanted to stop being a Mermaid; it was wrenched away.

"Wake up," she heard herself whisper to Gideon.

She did not know what else to do.

GRUMBACHER HAD the grace to look repentant. He stood a safe distance from Meredith and Gideon. Meredith sat at the edge of the bed, staring at the floor and wondering what to make of his silence.

Behind him, Appleby lurked by the door. He stared at her with the concern one might give a wounded animal.

"Well," Grumbacher managed, his tone not victorious as she would have expected, "I said it would not kill you."

Meredith shivered. She wished she was still Lady Meredith, ready with a cutting remark. Perhaps Lady Meredith had been the Mermaid; nothing remained of that fire.

A gleam on the bedside table caught her eye. Turning, she saw her mother's string of pearls. Agnes must have left them there after changing her. They provided familiarity. Reaching for the pearls, she counted them, trying to think of a response.

None came.

Appleby spoke. "Is your vision clear?"

"Yes," she said. Ten beads, twelve, fifteen—she could see them all.

"And your memory? Can you tell me your full name?"

"I can," she said icily, "but I won't."

Twenty beads, thirty—and she lost count. Frustrated, she began again, touching each bead, feeling its cool surface against her skin.

"Questions must be asked to be sure there aren't symptoms," Appleby said.

Meredith saw Grumbacher cringe and was tempted to feel sorry. She would not like to have a pest in her home, making decisions and speaking as if it were his.

"I don't owe either of you anything." She turned away to address Grumbacher. It was easier; his discomfort was proof that some form of soul remained. "You took from me without asking. Let me go."

Grumbacher shifted uneasily. Meredith had not been glaring, lacking the energy; it must be the truth that made him so wretched. She expected him to go up in flames, but did not care to be a witness. It would not return what had been taken.

"You should be monitored until you are stable," said Appleby with disdain. "Recovery—"

"Enough," barked Gideon, causing them all to jump. He

had been motionless on the chair for so long that he could have passed for a statue.

Gideon rose. Meredith saw Grumbacher cringe under his stare and was glad not to be in his place.

"I never thought you would sink to this," he said to his father. "Your business has always been pathetic, Silas, exploiting interesting things for money. At least in the past you did not hurt them. You could treat a strange bird with dignity. When did you sell yourself to this little serpent? Instead of bringing attention to interesting things, you degrade them."

Grumbacher inhaled as if to speak, but his voice reminded her of a mangled creature. Behind him, Appleby glowered.

Gideon continued. "I see you, Silas. I see the rot on your spirit. You did not expect for this treatment to be a success. You've become so accustomed to Merpeople dying that you never considered how to behave if this *cure* succeeded." He smiled with no cheer. "You're sorry because you see her now. You know that *with* or *without* Mermaid blood, she is perfect. You have given away your money, your house, your dignity."

Perfect? Meredith swallowed a lump in her throat.

"We're leaving," Gideon said, backing away. "She will recover somewhere else. There is nothing you or this *snake* can do to make it better." He spat the word like poison.

"Do you need anything?" Grumbacher managed, words hollow to match his eyes.

"One moment," Appleby said, as it sank in that Grumbacher did not plan to keep them. "This is not wise—"

Rounding on him, Grumbacher barked, "Enough! This is not your conversation, Appleby. Leave the room."

"You want to leave it unfinished! She might be—"

"Leave."

Appleby glowered, stalking off with an air that promised a row to come. As his footsteps faded, Meredith was able to breathe again, but did not lift her eyes.

She counted the pearls in her hand. *Perfect?* When had she been perfect? Her life had been a matter of making up for imperfections…

"How much do you think you will need?" Grumbacher asked, his face that of a tired old man. "You hardly have enough to support yourself."

"Your money is tainted by the deaths your experiment will cause," said Gideon. "I'll make my own living."

"You'll need a horse," was the reply, "if you intend to get anywhere today, Greer."

There might have been a nonverbal agreement; Meredith did not notice, fixated on her pearls. She did not look up until Gideon offered her a hand.

She would be a fool to deny that he believed his words true. He loved her, and he believed her to be perfect.

"Come," he said, "pack what you can carry."

GIDEON WAITED in the sitting room while Meredith went to pack. She stepped into her former bedroom, locking the door. The place looked bigger than it had the last time, or perhaps the treatment had made her smaller.

Shrugging off the sleeping gown, she stepped in front of the mirror and stared at her reflection. Scales fell to the ground, revealing smooth human skin.

She'd dreamt of losing teeth, but always woke to find

them healthy. Meredith shivered; she was wide awake, watching herself fall to the ground.

She dug a new frock out of the wardrobe and pulled it on. Then she found a canvas bag in her trunk, wondering what she ought to pack that could be of any help.

Mother's jewels provided security. Meredith emptied the contents of her trick box into the bag. She placed Gideon's folded note among the bracelets and earrings. Over the treasures she dropped a comb and a change of clothes.

No matter how she filled the bag, her emptiness remained.

She worked until interrupted by a knock at the door. Meredith considered ignoring it, but did not know what it would achieve. There was not much more they could do to her. Besides, they would have had to get past Gideon, so there was a fair chance it wasn't Appleby.

Agnes stood in the corridor, holding a journal. It had suffered a great deal in water, for the pages were frail and caught together, ink staining the edges.

The maid did not attempt to speak. She held it out, the meaning clear: *Take it and tell no one.*

Meredith hugged herself, remembering the afternoon she was given poisoned tea. Grumbacher boasted of finding a Mermaid cure in a journal. It washed up from a ship-wreck…it would be damaged by water.

"He did it to you, too," whispered Meredith. "You were a Mermaid."

Meredith's anger mingled with pity. Gideon said he suspected Agnes *wouldn't* talk, not that she *couldn't*. A scar had been made in her so deep that she would not raise her voice.

Agnes made no effort to confirm her suspicion.

Meredith took the journal, understanding. Whether it was true or not, nothing remained for the woman in front of her, no repair or freedom.

"Thank you," Meredith said, tucking the book under an arm.

Agnes managed a half-smile. She turned, slipping down the hall so lightly that not a floorboard creaked.

Bewildered, Meredith wrapped the journal in a scarf, pushing it towards the bottom of her bag. She would work out what to do with it later.

There remained the matter of leaving before Grumbacher lost what remained of his soul.

Thirty-One

PETER FOUND THE MOORES' HOME TO BE EXTREMELY QUIET. He must have spent too much time in Mrs. Whittle's chaotic orphanage. Trailing behind Rose, he listened to her speak to the girl with enthusiasm.

"We should not stay long," she said, "but it would be lovely to see the Moores and thank them."

"Very good, Miss Rose," said the maid. "Wait here. I will tell them."

She beckoned them into a sitting room. The curtains had been flung aside; light poured through the window onto gently-used cream chairs.

Peter kept silent as he sat, wondering how the Moores would greet him. It was important to thank them for having cared for his horse, but did they expect him to come? Would they be happy to see him? It might have been quicker to take the horse and leave a note of gratitude.

Rose looked with wonder at a painting over the mantel. It depicted a lighthouse on a pale winter's day. "I have never been past their front door," she said.

A series of questions went through his mind; he chose to ask the most pressing. "They might ask why you are leaving. What should we tell them?"

"The truth would be simple enough," Rose said. "There's no need to complicate things."

He could not resist a smile. "You're going to tell them I slept in the cellar and lurked in the kitchen until you agreed to come with me?"

"No, dear, that would be ridiculous," Rose said, taking a throw pillow and admiring its embroidery. "I'll tell them that I bullied you into proposing to me."

"That's more like it," he said, smirking.

It did not matter how they phrased their tale; Peter himself would have been skeptical if those events had not happened to him. The circumstances in which they met, the truths that came to light! He did not expect everybody to believe them.

Footsteps approached. He heard a man and a woman speaking in low voices.

"...wondered if he would say hello," the man said.

"Yes, I was rather hoping that he would."

Peter stood to greet their hosts. Mr. and Mrs. Moore joined them, both with smiles. Perhaps they had not expected him to visit, but they did not seem unhappy about it.

"Thank you for coming," said Mr. Moore, shaking his hand with enthusiasm. "I had begun to wonder if you left without the horse."

Peter smiled. Even if he could leave without the horse, he would not have done it. The disoriented steed had caused him to become lost in the best way.

"I hope she behaved well," he said. "I would have liked to

visit earlier, but Jimmy and Mrs. Whittle told me it was best to remain invisible."

"They might have been right," said Mr. Moore. "Not to worry; she is a calm steed. The money you sent our way was enough to keep her fed."

"Thank you for looking after her."

Mrs. Moore played with her pendant, a pretty bit of colored sea glass on a silver chain. "It was a surprise when Mrs. Whittle said that the horse belonged to you. We were saddened to read of your father's passing. We do get the newspapers, you know, our home being nearest to the border. It explained why Lord David stopped writing."

Peter did not like speaking of his father in the past tense, but was relieved that they knew the truth. It meant he would not have to explain Father's disappearance.

"The sinking of the *August* was too much for him," he said.

"An acquaintance who witnessed the wreck showed us some drawings of it," Mr. Moore said. "He said it was a pathetic sight—goods washing ashore, people stealing items. The greatest loss, though, is of life. I'm terribly sorry about it."

"Thank you. He is missed."

"Did you know that your father came regularly when he was your age?" Mrs. Moore asked. "His visits stopped after the death of Lord Finch. We began to wonder if he had forgotten about us."

"He did not say much about his younger years." Peter wished fiercely that he could have taken the time to ask questions; there were many things he would never learn. "I assure you, he was not the sort to forget old friends. He married and became occupied with other things."

"Did this place meet your expectations?"

"I didn't have expectations," he said sheepishly. "I didn't know I would turn up here."

"Not ever?" asked Mr. Moore with surprise.

"I would be lying if I told you I planned to come. It appears that fate intervened."

Mrs. Moore looked at Rose, who had been staring at her hands. There was a pause in which he felt the woman make a connection. Lifting her eyebrows, she said, "You're going with him, *Lady Rose*."

She used the title in a probing way, a gentle attempt to dig for truth.

Rose's eyes widened. "How long have you known?" she whispered.

"Your mother never seemed to belong in this place. Even when dressed simply, she held herself as someone genteel. When no one said a thing, we kept our suspicions to ourselves. After you became a part of the community, there was no reason to ask."

Rose's expression was impossible to read as she stared at the worn carpet. Peter knew that she was hurting, jarred by the discovery that her identity had not been such a secret. She might be wishing that the Moores could have broken their silence. Their intervention might have helped her leave sooner.

If indeed she was disappointed, she said nothing of it. Instead, she said, "The time has come for me to return. I would like to make peace with the place where I was born."

"Good luck, Lady Rose," said Mrs. Moore. "Your secret will be safe with us until you reveal it yourself."

Rose nodded, clasping her hands on her lap—a sign of tension, Peter knew. He hoped that the visit would end soon. The prospect of returning home might be daunting, but at least he knew the people there.

"Please don't tell anyone yet," said Rose. "I will write to Mrs. Whittle with updates."

Mrs. Moore looked from Rose to Peter. "You will write to us when there is a date for the wedding?" she asked. "We'll find a way to attend."

"Of course," Rose said, reddening sweetly as she glanced at Peter.

Mrs. Moore beamed. "You're a lovely pair."

A clock in the corridor chimed, putting an end to the exchange.

"If you're leaving, it should not be too late," said Mr. Moore. "Let's go to the stable."

Peter was glad to see his horse, though he wished he knew her name. As he fixed a borrowed saddle on her, he regretted not knowing what to call the mare.

"It'll be a long journey for one horse to carry two people," said Mr. Moore dubiously. "I'll loan you our youngest, Sunny. She isn't fast, but I am sure she won't mind a journey."

"It's kind of you to offer her," Peter said. "I haven't any form of payment, though."

"Your father was a friend of mine. I trust you to keep her safe."

Mr. Moore neared a light-brown horse with a white patch on her face. True to her name, Sunny blinked at him as she basked in the morning light.

My father is helping, Peter thought with wonder, *though he is not here.*

It felt surreal when, minutes later, they set off back to civilization.

Rose's unease had faded; she was comfortable and confident, steering Sunny with steady hands. Peter searched her face for regret, but saw only raw determination.

Peter felt a stab of disappointment that he had not seen the ocean-bound Merpeople. Though he did not blame them for choosing to maintain their privacy, curiosity caused him to look over his shoulder, hoping for a glimpse.

Rose followed his gaze. "I'm sure they'll appear next time," she said.

"If they choose not to, I understand." He did not believe his own words. If Father and Lord Julian had been friends of the Mer, why did their sea-bound relatives not trust him?

"Oh, they will," she said optimistically. "Don't put much faith in the Moores' ability to keep a secret. Word travels fast, and it will also reach the sea."

"That sounds like a threat," Peter said, smiling.

Rose urged Sunny forward, her turquoise eyes sparkling like the ocean behind them. "Soon I won't be a secret, either," she reminded him. "I'm beginning to think it will be fun."

Peter allowed her to take the lead, grappling with disbelief. At some point, his stubbornness had convinced her that it would not be so bad to return home.

Rose's word choice caused his smile to widen. *Fun* was an idea he very much needed to relearn. He would follow her example as he reclaimed his life.

A disaster waited at the end of their journey. He would try to enjoy the process of tidying it up.

Thirty-Two

ROSE TRIED NOT TO DWELL ON HOW FAR THE DIRT PATH WAS taking her from the orphanage.

She imagined the girls growing up without her. Marie would take responsibility over their lessons, ensuring that they did not become idle. With her, Mrs. Whittle would have a helping hand in all things.

Rose told herself that it was a good thing. They could not depend on her to manage an entire house. It was time for her to assume new responsibilities elsewhere. Though Peter tried to appear brave, she saw his unease about facing his family.

Peter's uncle might be kind, but an exchange was bound to happen. She chose to be by his side, even if she could do little more than listen.

"There are buildings ahead," said Peter, breaking a long silence. "I recognize this place. My uncle's house is not far."

"Does this mean our journey is over?"

"The simple part, at least." He exhaled, a long and slow breath. "There are shops here that sell clothing; I would like to clean up. I'd also like to send him a note. It would be rude to catch him off-guard."

Rose glanced at her own tattered frock, wondering what Theodore would think of her appearance. Noticing her glance, Peter beamed.

"You can also choose something while we await a reply," he said—and something in his tone caused her to blush.

"You don't have to spend money on a frock," Rose mumbled, nudging Sunny over a fence, turning away to conceal her pink cheeks.

"Why not?" Peter quipped, following suit. When she could not form a reply, he added gently, "If it makes you more comfortable, consider this a gift of thanks for all of the time you tolerated me in the kitchen."

Rose held her breath, nodding once. Her appearance was not only a matter of vanity. A tense conversation awaited them at Theodore's house; it was important that she should look presentable.

"There's the bank. Do you mind waiting here? They will know who I am, but I don't want to waste time explaining things."

"Explaining that I am not dead?" she asked, smiling. "Of course I'll wait."

Rose steered Sunny to the shade of a tree and took the reins of Peter's horse. She watched as he walked into the bank. If he was right, and they knew who he was, gossip would soon be circulating.

Society never changed; those who spread rumors were merciless. It was one thing she hadn't missed while working for Mrs. Whittle.

Finished with the withdrawal, Peter paid a boy to deliver a note to his uncle. They then searched for a clothing-shop, tethering their horses to a fence before approaching the door.

"Was the note necessary?" Rose asked, linking her arm with his. "You said he has a better temperament."

"I would still give him time to reflect," said Peter.

"You think that he is angry with you?"

"I wouldn't blame him if he was."

"Perhaps you're thinking about it the wrong way. What if he isn't angry, but worried? Your life is more important than a reputation."

Peter shrugged his shoulders, pressed a kiss to her hand. "There's only one way to find out."

He opened the shop door, stepping aside. Entering, Rose was blinded by the colors and fabrics. Gowns were on display of such a quality that she had not seen in years. Those she inherited from Mother were threadbare from overuse. She had left them in the wardrobe for Marie, hoping her friend would enjoy them.

"This place is familiar," Peter said. "I've accompanied Sybil here in the past."

A woman stepped forward and asked, "How can we be of assistance, My Lord?"

Her eyes lingered on Rose, something eerily knowing in her smile. Those in the business of gossip missed nothing.

"Lady Rose would like something appropriate for a house call," Peter said, eyes narrowing—he had noticed the look, as well.

The assistants slowed what they were doing when Peter said her name. They stared as if they had no doubts of which Lady Rose she was. She found it strange—Rose was a common name!

"Very good, sir," said the woman. "Lucy will help you, My Lady."

"Thank you."

Rose followed the assistant named Lucy to the back, where several gowns were on display. She admired the shades of blue and red, swallowing a knot in her throat. Marie would have loved to shop with her.

"That blue one, I think," she said, deciding on the comfort of her favorite color. Turning to Lucy, she asked, "Could somebody help me with my hair? I'm afraid it came undone in the wind."

"I can fix hair," said Lucy. "If this is your choice, My Lady, we'll step into the back and get you dressed."

After a sponge bath, she was fitted into new under-clothes. With great care, Lucy helped her into the dress. Its soft, clean fabric felt alien to her skin.

Rose was not oblivious to Lucy's questions about her past.

"Will Countless Arabella shop here?" she asked. "Mother says she was a favorite customer—all colors perfect on her!"

"Yes, all colors," Rose said with a smile, then changed the subject with haste. "I was taken by your variety. Perhaps I will return."

"Mother owns the shop. We would be honored to have you again!"

"Splendid," Rose said.

"Lady Sybil frequents this place," Lucy added. "She comes with her friends."

Rose's heart ached at the thought of Sybil. Would they be friends, or had Sybil changed during their separation?

Lucy continued to babble, weaving Rose's hair into an

elaborate braid. Rose did not pay attention to her speech, dozing, until a familiar name was mentioned.

"Lady Meredith also shopped here. It's a shame that she married and went away. She's sure to have found other places for clothing."

Rose was struck with curiosity about the woman who hurt Peter. Lucy's claim seemed odd. It had not been long since that party; had Lady Meredith already married elsewhere?

Rose decided to ask questions, hoping to learn more. "How was the wedding? I'm afraid I was not invited."

"No one that we know attended," Lucy said. "It was a private event. If not for an announcement in the paper, I would not have known. Lady Sybil was furious that Lady Meredith was married so soon after..."

The girl stopped, but Rose could guess what she was about to say. *After what happened with Lord Peter.*

"I forgot the name of the man she married," Rose told Lucy, feigning a tired smile.

"Oh, it's some foreign name—grim...grim...no, grum—*Grumbacher!*" Lucy said. "The owner of the famous museum of oddities. Have you seen the two-headed mummy? What a grim collection!"

"Yes," Rose lied. "I have seen it. Oh, Lucy, thank you—my journey was tiring, and I appreciate your help."

"My Lady," said Lucy, dipping into a curtsy. "We await your return."

Standing, Rose looked into the full-length mirror. A younger version of Mother stared back at her. Before Arabella became ill, people commented that she and her daughter were similar in appearance.

Again, she pined for Marie's presence. Marie would

enjoy work at a place like this! She had the taste to transform any woman into a princess, but lacked resources.

"I have a friend who might enjoy employment here," she said. "I will ask her and write back to you."

"Delighted, My Lady," said Lucy.

Rose rubbed warmth into her hands before opening the door and stepping back into the shop. She could not explain to herself why Peter's reaction to her appearance mattered so very much.

He stood by the window, staring at the afternoon sun. Already he had changed into a blue suit with silver cufflinks. His hair had been combed into place.

He looked like this, Rose thought, *before he fell off that horse.*

She took a step nearer. "Fortunate of you," she said, "that you're already finished."

Peter turned. Rose smiled—he looked like the prince she had imagined all along.

"Will this do for a resurrection?" she jested. "I wouldn't want to embarrass you."

"Lady Rose," he began, "I..."

Before he could finish speaking, a hansom cab rattled up the street, stopping in front of the store. She saw disappointment in Peter's face. "That's my uncle's," he said. "I hoped we would have time for tea next door."

"Another day," she said, though her heart also sank. How much time would pass before they could go someplace else alone?

He offered an arm; she took it, wondering if he could hear her heart thumping against her chest.

To the woman at the desk he said, "Send the bill to Theodore West's house. It'll be paid in the morning."

"Yes, My Lord," agreed the woman, curtsying. To Rose she said, "Thank you for coming, Lady Rose."

The driver held the cab door for them. She stepped in, hugging her bag to her chest. Peter gave orders that their horses should be attached to the cab before joining her.

Rose noticed that his breath was unsteady. The change of appearance had not lightened his nerves.

As the cab rattled into movement, she whispered into his ear, "Peter, I thought you should know. Lucy, the assistant— she said to me—that the woman you almost married—has married someone else."

The words jolted him back to reality. "Already?" he asked with disbelief. "To whom?"

She told him all that she had heard as the cab pulled away from the shops, into a path through the woods. Even as she whispered of that woman, she noticed that he did not release her hand—and wondered if he noticed how tightly he held her.

Rose was glad; she did not want to release him, either.

Thirty-Three

THE MOTION OF A MOVING HORSE DENIED MEREDITH THE sleep that her body longed for, yet she was not alert. She did not notice Gideon slipping off of the horse. When later she opened her eyes, she was surprised to find him walking contentedly beside her.

Meredith squinted over her shoulder. Ill as she was, she feared Grumbacher House might appear in the distance. Her face and neck were warm with fever; she could not gather her thoughts.

"What time is it?" she asked. The sky was darker than it had been when she nodded off.

"Late afternoon," Gideon said, glancing at a battered pocket-watch. "The process of packing and leaving stalled us."

He was too kind to say that she was to blame for their delay. If he hadn't been chivalrous and left her alone on the horse, they would be halfway across the plains.

"You shouldn't have to walk, Mr. Greer," she said.

"I like walking," said Gideon. "A storm is coming, My

Lady. If we don't find shelter, we'll be soaked *and* late. There's a barn coming up that ought to keep us from the worst of it."

Meredith did not answer. His smile might have been honest, but she could no longer see the world with optimism. If not for her, Gideon would have arrived at the village. He would be indoors, not finding shelter in a barn.

She did not disdain the barn. A barn was better than the mansion in which she had been raised. It was warmer than the house where she was sent away to be poked at and prodded, where half of her had been killed.

Meredith's soul protested that Gideon should be in a barn because of her. She was tired of bringing misfortune to others.

"It's straight ahead," said Gideon.

The barn's appearance did not bring comfort. It wasn't cozy like those in paintings. There were so many holes in the roof that she doubted its efficiency against a storm. However, the gray clouds were thick enough that she saw no point in arguing.

"In you go," Gideon told the horse, who ambled gratefully to shelter. "You're all of the inheritance I'm going to get." He somehow managed to make that sound cheerful.

The horse nodded her head, dark eyes full of understanding. Gideon gave her a pat and received an affectionate nudge.

Meredith had read that some people communicated with animals. She never tried; feral cats and starved dogs shied from her glare. As she watched Gideon converse with his horse, it dawned on her that she could not communicate with humans, either.

"Right," Gideon said to Meredith. "I'll help you down."

A bit of pride reared up. She wanted to retort that she *did not* need help. Logic set in, reminding her that every time she tried to help herself, she got into more trouble. Reluctantly she accepted his hand and slid off the horse, stumbling when she landed on her feet.

Gideon's grip on her tightened. "All right?"

Meredith did not reply, angry with something she could not name. Countless thoughts raged through her mind; if only she could sort through them. If only she knew what made her angry, she might be able to take a breath.

"I need to sleep," she managed.

In sleep, she might sort out what was bothering her. In sleep, she could forget who she was—what she no longer was...

"Get up to the loft," said Gideon. "It's going to rain. The ground will be sodden, and you've got a temperature."

Meredith looked at the loft. It might have been impressive when new; now she preferred to stay on ground level. "There will be rats."

"There are rats here, too," he said.

"And spiders."

He exhaled. *Of course*, thought Meredith, backing away, *he will have more patience with a horse than me.*

"Fine. Sleep here," he said, something like sadness in his tone. "I'm used to places like this, but I understand that you're not. We'll leave when the storm passes."

Meredith watched him clear a spot, spreading a blanket over it. In truth, she did not care about rats or spiders. She had endured enough in life that the thought of a bite no longer caused her dread.

Rats wanted food and did not pretend otherwise. They never cared what she was or if her heritage was tainted.

Monsters lived in great houses, dressed in finery, using intelligence to do wicked things.

She struggled to understand Gideon. He was too kind for a man who had found himself homeless on her behalf. Perhaps he did not yet realize all that he lost. He might regret defending her after several days of sleeping in barns.

If he should find out the sort of person she was, the atrocities she had done, would his kindness vanish? Meredith did not think it fair that he should be oblivious to her sins. She would find an opportunity to tell him, but not yet. She did not have the energy for such a conversation.

Gideon looked at the blanket. "It'll be prickly, but I imagine you won't notice once you're asleep."

Meredith smiled. She felt no mirth, but did not trust herself to speak with kindness. Her vision blurred; the fever had not broken.

"Have some water," he said. "I think I packed enough."

Gideon took a jar from his threadbare bag. He opened it and held it out, smiling. The expression might have charmed a horse with no consciousness, but Meredith only felt uncomfortable.

"It's yours," she said, looking at the water. "You packed it."

"I'm offering it to you," he said. "Soon there'll be a stream to replenish it."

Meredith continued to stare. It would be fresh water, of course—no salt. Her body did not want water from the ocean, yet the thought of fresh water triggered panic. Fresh water stirred memories of a childhood shaded by punishment. Caught between worlds, she would never find peace...

"Meredith?" Gideon asked. "What is it?"

"Nothing," she said, walking towards the blanket. "Only —only a memory."

He took her arm and said, "If you don't speak of it, the memory will haunt you. I learned that myself."

She resisted. The act of holding a secret gave her power. Mentally, she stood on a precipice. The Mermaid had been killed; if she released the truth, what would prevent the rest of her from vanishing?

"I'll drink water," she whispered, shying from the subject.

Gideon took a breath as if to argue, but stopped himself. He handed her the jar.

Meredith took slow sips, trying to ignore the pure taste. She swallowed half of the jar before stopping. Pure water tasted like punishment, deprivation.

Outside, the grass rustled as raindrops began to fall. A question remained in Gideon's expression. Ignoring it, Meredith sat on the blanket. She closed her eyes, listening to the sky burst open.

In the stillness, she felt Gideon sit beside her. He waited for her to speak. He seemed to take seriously the saying that, with persistence, any creature would confide.

"Thank you for the water," was all that she said.

The rain increased in speed. Meredith could smell the damp as a downpour began. Soon she would feel it in her bones.

"I can't help if you won't tell me what's bothering you," Gideon said, relentless.

A raindrop slipped through the roof, landing on some nearby hay. Meredith waited for another to follow, staring at the spot with bated breath.

"You can't help me," she whispered.

"You won't convince me that I can't do anything."

For a breathless second she heard in his voice a boy who wanted to prove himself. It caused her to smile, such an honest sound. He was the first person in her life to show himself for what he was, persistent in little things.

"You can't," Meredith said, "and neither can I." She felt herself dissolve like the sky above them, flashes of lightning striking her heart as a rumble rose in the air. "Grumbacher let me go, but I don't know what he put into me."

No one had deigned to tell her what was in the treatment, the contents of the syringe. She would never have a peaceful life; for all that she knew, poison pulsed through her, waiting to take her in sleep.

Fear paralyzed her on the ground.

Meredith closed her eyes, wishing the rain could wash her insides clean.

She was relieved when Gideon did not ask more questions, and pitied him. He had no choice but to lug her with him through an uncertain life–she, Meredith Bannister.

No longer a lady, no longer a Mermaid. As far as she was concerned, no longer a Bannister.

Nothing but an empty shell.

To Be Continued...

About the Author

Based in the Treasure Valley, Mariella Hunt writes clean fantasy novels featuring a dash of magic. Her favorite authors are the classics: Austen, Dickens, and Montgomery are only a few of her heroes. To this day, she is not convinced that Merpeople don't exist.

90849782R00149